The Return of Nemesis
Nate the Great!

The Return of Nemesis
Nate the Great!

Shannon Gaffney McCall

Cover Art by: Nicole Brekelbaum

AuthorHouse™ LLC
1663 Liberty Drive
Bloomington, IN 47403
www.authorhouse.com
Phone: 1-800-839-8640

Published by AuthorHouse   02/24/2014

ISBN: 978-1-4918-6370-1 (sc)
ISBN: 978-1-4918-6482-1 (e)

Library of Congress Control Number: 2014902897

Dedicated to the apples of my eye, my sons, Rashod and Andrew.

The Andrews and Gaffney families grew stronger. As Eva the Grandma Diva liked to quote," A family that prays together stays together!" Prayer and church had become a constant and uplifting part of their lives. As a matter of fact, one Sunday afternoon while they shared one of their legendary family dinners, there was a firm knock on the front door.

"I'll get it!" declares Nathan, excusing himself from the table.

He opened the door and there stood a tall, slim, well-dressed man with Nathan's complexion and Ola Mae's eyes, twinkle and all.

"Can I help you, sir?" Nate inquires politely.

"I believe you sure can," replies the man, smiling as he peers into the boy's eyes, "I'm here to see my son . . . Nathan!"

"Dad!" Nathan exclaims, crying tears of joy as he hugs his long lost father, "Me'ma told me to tell you that she forgives you . . . and I do too!"

Excerpt from Max & Lucy

CHAPTER ONE

Reunited and Excited!

"Max, everybody, come meet my dad!" Nathan yells, excitedly tugging his father into the house.

The family hurried to the living room to see what all the commotion was about. One by one Nate introduced his foster family to his biological father, Nathaniel Campbell.

The news was very overwhelming to them. Although the question weighing heavy on everyone's mind was *"Where the heck have you been,"* no one dared to ask. Instead they excuse themselves to give Nathan and Nathaniel time to begin getting to know each other.

"There are so many things I want to tell you. I don't know where to start," stammers Nathan, beyond excited that he and his father have been reunited.

"How about you start by telling me how you've been since your Me'ma passed?"

Nate sat quietly. To think of Ola Mae made him both happy and sad. Remembering how she loved him dearly caused him ache inside that she was gone.

"Me'ma lives on in my heart. I'm sad she died but she was suffering. And in a way, I think she knew she was going to die because she found a family to take care of me, this family . . . the Andrews."

"They seem like nice people."

"They are the best. You'll see once you get to know them. Right now I want to know what happened? Why did you leave me with Me'ma and disappear? We needed you," Nathan says getting straight to the point.

Tears gloss Nathaniel's eyes and Nathan sits patiently awaiting his father's explanation.

"Son, it's like this. You don't go from being a boy to a man overnight. Growing in age doesn't make you a man. The same is true about being a dad. Having a baby . . . becoming a parent . . . doesn't make you a *dad*. It's hard to explain, but being a parent and being a dad are two totally different things. When you are older you will understand."

Nate looks at his father, confused. "You still didn't answer my question. Why did you leave me?"

Nathaniel sits up straight, clears his throat and looks his son square in the eye. "I had growing up to do. It had nothing to do with you or my love for you. I loved you enough to do what was best for you.

Without your mother, I was only a shell of a man. I left you with your Me'ma because I knew she could give you what I couldn't at the time. Your grandmother had always been an angel, even before death gave her wings. Nathan, I had to grow into manhood. I hope one day you understand."

Father and son stared at each other in silence. Nathan had so many other questions, he didn't know what to ask next. Nathaniel, on the other hand, didn't have all the answers but hoped they would come to him as his son asked.

"Honestly dad, I don't exactly know what you mean. All I do know is I am so glad you came back."

"Me too, Nathan. I missed you and Me'ma more than you'll ever know."

"Where have you been? Are you moving here?"

Nathaniel rises and kneels down in front of the chair Nate is sitting in. "I came to take you back with me to New York."

Nathan was both thrilled and distressed. He had really begun to love having a family. He hated the thought of leaving the Andrews, especially Max. But New York was big, with big city lights and he was anxious to see all the sites.

"New York? You've been in New York all this time?"

"Yes, son in one sense or another. Look Nathan, there is going to be plenty of time to get to know each other and ample time for me to answer your questions. We have the rest of our lives to play catch-up. Right now I need to know one thing. Do you want to come home with me or would you like to stay here with the Andrews family?

If you want to stay I will understand. They can provide you with so much more than I can. Here with them you have it all, a very nice home, access to the finest things money can buy, not to mention a family atmosphere. In New York it will just be you and me. I don't have the fanciest apartment, but I believe it will suit us fine. I can't give you *everything* you want, but I will be able to give you *some* of them, although, it may take a little while. The choice is yours Nathan. I want you to be happy even if that means not living with me. I feel I owe you that much."

"I want to go back to New York with you!" Nate cries out, clinging to his father. "Please never leave me again!"

"I promise Nathan, I'll *never* leave you again. Nothing in this world can make me leave you."

"Can we stay here a week or so before we go?"

"I do have a few things to take care here before I can legally take you back with me. But I don't know if we will be able to stay a few weeks. I can't be away from my business that long."

"Okay. Let's go tell the others the news . . . *New York?* Wow!"

Nathaniel waited as his son rounded up his foster family. He felt very nervous and guilty as well. He tried to come up with a simple yet reasonable explanation for his absence, hoping the question would not arise.

The Andrews family gathered in the living room and tried to be very courteous. Everyone shook Nathaniel's hand as Nate introduced them again, everyone except Eva of course.

"Oh no you don't!" she exclaims, slapping his hand down. "If you are family to Nathan, you are family to us. You better give me a hug!"

The whole family burst into laughter.

"That's Granny for you," whispers Max to Nathan.

"Where are you staying?" asks Eva, the Grandma Diva.

"In town at the Holiday Inn."

"Oh no, we can't have that. Family stays with family around here. So you just go on to that hotel and get your bags. I'll turn down the extra bed for you."

Nathaniel smiles eerily.

It had been twelve years since he has been in the Deep South.

Shannon Gaffney McCall

He had forgotten all about Southern hospitality. People in New York were so rude and uncaring. Everyone shuffling to their own beat, consumed by their own little worlds, giving very little thought to the existence of others.

"I couldn't possibly impose on ya'll like that. I wouldn't feel right."

"I have to step in now," interjects Dr. Andrews, "You will not be imposing. We insist. Please, we have more than enough room. Plus take it from me, my mama is not going to take no for an answer."

"Please!" adds Nathan.

"Please, Mr. Campbell. I want to spend as much time as I can with Nate before ya'll leave," begs Max.

"Yeah, dad I want to be close to Lucky and Sam, too. You said you live in an apartment and I know we can't have a dog there, can we?"

Nathaniel was clearly backed into a corner. He had so much to make-up to Nathan that he decided there's no better time to start than the present.

"You are right. You can't have a dog in the apartment. So I guess, _only_ if you don't have to go through any extra trouble on my behalf, I will stay here."

"Thanks," yells Nate.

The others look at them and smile. With all of them happy, Nathan is finally sampling true joy.

"It's no trouble at all," says Mary Andrews. "We're glad to have you."

"Well, what are you waiting for? Go get your bags from that hotel," demands Eva.

"My suitcase is outside in my rental car. I couldn't wait a second longer than necessary to see Nathan. It has already been too long. So I stopped by here before going to check into the hotel. I pedaled that poor rental car as fast as it would go to get here from the airport in Atlanta."

"Good! You boys go get Mr. Campbell's suitcase!"

"Please, call me Nathaniel."

"Okay, well you boys go get _Nathaniel's_ suitcase," she repeats to Nate and Max.

"Can we go out back and play with the puppies afterwards?" inquires Nate.

4

"That's between you and your father," replies Eva.

Nathaniel nods his approval.

"Mary, you and Suzann go turn down the bed in the extra bedroom and then come help me in the kitchen. We are going to show Nathaniel what he's been missing up there in Slick City, down-home cooking."

"What can I do?" whines little Olivia.

Eva bends over to talk to the child on her level. "You can come in the kitchen with me, and if you are real good you can lick the spoon when I make my famous chocolate cake."

"I'll be tha best!" says Olivia, skipping towards the kitchen.

"We are going to leave you men to talk," declares Eva, following after the family's youngest.

As soon as the coast was clear, Dr. Maxwell Andrews apologizes for his mother's bossiness. "That's just the way she is, at large and in charge! She doesn't mean any harm."

"No need to apologize. As you know, my mama was just as blunt as the top of a baseball bat."

Maxwell smiles as he thinks about Ola Mae Campbell. "She was such a sweet lady. Ola Mae truly had a heart of gold and a wise sparkle in her eye."

"I missed her so much, but things happened that prevented me from coming back," confesses Nathaniel.

"Trust me, you don't owe us any explanation!"

"Oh, but I feel I really do," says Nathaniel, embarrassed. "You've been doing what I was supposed to be doing. You helped my mother and have been caring for my son since her death. I owe you so much and I'm prepared to reimburse you the cost of Mama's funeral."

"Don't be silly, Nathaniel. The only thing I want from you is for you to take very good care of Nathan. He's a real special boy who has come a long way from the very first time I met him."

"I see why Mama chose ya'll for Nathan. You're going to be a tough act to follow."

"Trust me, Nathaniel, Nathan would be happy with you living in a cardboard box. That young man longs for nothing more than your presence," assures Al.

"I promise you, I'm going to do everything I can to make this up to him. And I will never keep him from ya'll. You are truly his family, the only family he's ever known."

"What are you talking about *his* family? You are family too. If the Andrews-Gaffney's don't stand for anything else, we stand for family," Maxwell states proudly.

"That's right. When it boils down to it, family is all you have in the end," adds Al.

Maxwell and Al spend the next couple of hours bringing Nathaniel up to speed, beginning with the uncanny and violent way Nathan and Max had first become acquainted. They enlightened him as to how that faithful Thanksgiving the previous year they became a blended family. They explained the reunion of Suzann and Mary. The discovery of Lucy and the pups she left behind. Maxwell even walked Nathaniel through Ola Mae's last days and how Nathan had come to live with them. By the time they finished, Nathaniel couldn't have felt more like family if they all shared blood.

"Dinner is served," Eva the Grandma Diva calls out two hours later. "Get washed up and let's eat."

Once everyone was seated around the dining room table hands adjoined, Eva insisted Nathaniel say the grace. He was uneasy at first, but Nathan squeezed his dad's hand in support.

"Heavenly Father, we thank You for the food that has been prepared. We pray that You bless the hands that prepared it and everyone who partakes. Lord, I thank You for this great family who has taken good care of my Nathan. And last but not least, I thank You for reuniting my son and me. Amen!"

"Amen!" the group says simultaneously.

The buffet before the family reminded Nathaniel of Sunday dinners when he was a child. Eva, Mary and Suzann had created quite a spread. There was potato salad, green beans, collard and mustard greens, long grain white rice, tender juicy Boston Butt with homemade brown gravy, baked macaroni and cheese, black eye peas, chicken and dumplings, buttery biscuits made from scratch, blueberry muffins, chocolate cake, peach cobbler, and sweet tea.

"I have to give it to you ladies, I haven't eaten this good since I left here. This food tastes even better than it smells," commends Nathaniel, devouring his entrees.

"You eat until your heart is content, honey. There's plenty!" says Eva.

"I know those New York women can't cook like this," declares Al, dipping himself a second helping of chicken and dumplings.

"Honestly," Nathaniel replies between bites, "I wouldn't know, but I bet you are right."

"Well, when you are ready, you come on back home and we'll find you a Georgia Peach too," says Eva, spooning another bowl of peach cobbler into Nathaniel's empty dessert dish. "Until then, you know where you can find a home-cooked meal."

"I'll keep that in mind."

After dinner, the women of the family put away the leftovers and cleaned the kitchen. Al and Maxwell retired to the new addition to the Andrews' home, known as the man-cave, to play cards. Max took Olivia to his room to attempt to teach her how to play Madden. And Nathan and Nathaniel walked Lucky and Sam to the park. Everyone wanted to give them some more alone time to bond.

"Well Nathan, I don't know where to begin. There's so much I've missed out on. How about school? Do you like school? What kind of grades do you make?"

He stops in his tracks, Nathan pauses before speaking.

"Nathan, son, you can tell me anything. Don't ever feel like you can't come to me with anything. I want to know it all, your joys and your pains, the good and the bad. I'm here for you now, Nate. All I ask is that you be honest with me at all times and I'm going to do the same."

Nathan believed his father. He believed he could tell his father anything and now that they were back together he felt there was nothing they could not overcome.

"I got in trouble at school. I was expelled. Aunt Suzann has been home schooling me. Honestly dad, I think being expelled was a blessing. Granny Eva always says there is a silver lining to every cloud.

Aunt Suzann takes the time to help me understand the schoolwork. She doesn't make me feel stupid if I don't get something right away. Me'ma tried her best to help me, but her eyes were bad. In fact, before she passed she was completely blind."

Nathaniel beamed within, knowing he has his son's complete trust. After all, he already knew Nathan had been expelled from school and was only testing the waters by asking.

"Sounds like Suzann's a great teacher."

"She really is. I'm going to really miss her. I'm going to really miss them all."

"I know you will, but you can visit. It's not like you'll never see them again. And just between you and me, your old man was not the best student in the world. And I'll never proclaim to be an angel either, so you got it honest."

The two begin walking towards the park once more. "What about Mom, was she a good student?" asks Nate.

"Nathan, your mother was great at everything she did. I wish you could have known her."

"Me too, dad, me too."

The rest of the journey to the park and back both father and son remain quiet. They were both imagining, as each had done countless times before, what it would be like if they had been a *complete* family, Abigail included.

When they return, the family is outside enjoying the evening breeze. "We thought you guys had gotten lost," jokes Eva.

"Yeah, I was about to call the station to put an B.O.L.O. (be on the lookout) on ya'll," laughs Al.

"Nah, it's been so long since I've smelled fresh air, we took our time and lavished in it. New York is so polluted."

"We 'bout to go get ice cream," gloats Olivia.

"Correction, Missy, we *might* go get some ice cream," declares Suzann, ushering her young daughter towards the Gaffney's S.U.V.

"But daddy!" pouts Olivia.

"Get in the truck and I'll work on Mommy for you," replies Al, winking at his stepdaughter.

"Everything is still a go for tomorrow, right Al?" inquires Maxwell.

"If Olivia and I aren't sharing the doghouse," he clowns, causing everyone to giggle, even Suzann, who is trying her best not to crack a smile.

"I'll call you with the details after I talk to Nathaniel and Nathan."

"Alright, you folks take it easy."

"Bye," Suzann and Olivia chime.

"I'm pretty sure you two are wondering what we are talking about," Maxwell says to Nathaniel and Nathan. "Well if you're game, we would like to go fishing tomorrow afternoon. Fathers and kids. No women, with the exception of Lil Olivia, of course," he announces, looking at his wife Mary and mother Eva.

"That sounds nice," declares Nathaniel.

"What is going to be nice is watching you men clean and cook the fish you catch. Since we women are not welcome to join you fishing, we will *not* join you in the preparation either. Now if you gentlemen will excuse me, I have a book deadline to meet," Mary chuckles going into the house.

Maxwell pleads to Eva with his eyes.

"Don't give me the puppy dog eyes. You set yourself up for that one. Don't fret. Your father taught you how to clean anything you could possibly catch, so you fellows will be just fine," she concludes, pinching her son's chin and entering the house too.

"It's been a while since I've been fishing. In fact I know the last time I went fishing was about five years *before* Nathan was born. So consider yourselves warned. I'm a bit rusty."

"Don't worry Nathaniel, it's like riding a bike. It'll all come back to you."

"Come on Nate, let's go to the garage and pick out the best reels." The adolescents charge for the garage.

"Can I ask you something serious?" inquires Nathaniel.

"Sure. Take a load off," suggests Maxwell, pointing to a wooden rocker. "Would you like a glass of lemonade?"

"No thank you, I'm fine."

"So what's on your mind?"

"Every parent wants to do what is best for their child."

"True."

"And I thought . . . no, I *know* leaving Nathan with my mama was the best thing for him all those years ago."

Maxwell listens attentively.

"Now that I'm here, I'm wondering if taking Nate back with me is truly what's best for him or if it's what best for my selfish heart. He has a real family here with ya'll, something I can't give him. What do you think?"

Maxwell thinks long and hard before he finally speaks. "We are a family, true enough. A family that was first joined by blood but is now joined by love. It didn't happen overnight, but when it happened it was well worth the ups and downs, not to mention all the effort that went into it. It wasn't easy but it was *worth* it. Look at Mary and Suzann."

"I get it. You're a wise man, Maxwell."

"Nah, I'm no more wise than the next guy. I'm a blessed man, a man lucky enough to share his life with some great people."

"I think I'll have a little lemonade now," Nathaniel says, finally comfortable with his decision to take Nathan back with him to New York.

"Here you are," says Maxwell, handing him a tall glass. "Who do you favor in the Super Bowl?"

Maxwell and Nathaniel talked about football, family, and life in general growing up as country boys until it was time to say goodnight to their sons. Just as their seeds had become the best of friends, the two men quickly realize the same could easily happen between them.

Late that night after everyone one was fast asleep, Nathan snuck downstairs to the spare bedroom where his father was sleeping. At first he sat quietly, Indian style, on the floor beside his father's bed. It seemed unreal, like a dream. For so many years he had yearned to sleep in the same house as his dad. Now he was only a few inches away from him. Nate wasn't exactly sure why he was sitting there watching his father sleep. He just knew it was a wonderful feeling.

"Nathan, I'm not going anywhere, at least not anywhere *without* you. So you don't have to watch me," whispers Nathaniel with his eyes still shut.

"I didn't mean to wake you."

"It's quite alright, son. I wasn't sleeping anyway, just resting my eyes."

Nathan smiles from the inside out, "Me'ma used to say that all the time."

Slowly Nathaniel opens his eyes, "You are so right, and if you hadn't brought it to my attention I wouldn't have even put one and two together. I guess *resting my eyes* is one of many things I picked up from her."

"Dad, can I rest my eyes with you?"

"Sure you can," Nathaniel replies.

Nate makes himself at home lying across the foot of his father's borrowed bed. "Thank you for coming back."

Nathaniel sits up and turns on the lamp near the bed. "Look at me, Nathan."

Nathan rolls over and faces his father.

"There wasn't a day that went by that I didn't think about you or wonder what and how you were doing. You were *always* in my thoughts and prayers."

Silent tears kiss Nathan's cheeks.

"Nathan, you said your grandma told you to tell me she forgave me."

"She did. I wouldn't lie about that."

"I believe you, son. I'm not questioning your sincerity. I want to know if *you* will forgive me?" Nathaniel admits, crying silent tears of his own.

"Daddy, of course I do I already told you that. I was never mad at you. I just don't understand what happened. But you said you had a good reason and I'll understand when I'm older. I'm taking your word for that. We are going to work through this together, right? Me'ma forgave you and so did I."

"I'd have it no other way. You and me 'til the end. You are my Sidekick through thick and thin."

"Sidekick. I like the sound of that. You have always been my invisible hero."

"And you have always been my Sidekick, by my side everywhere I went," Nathaniel announces, reaching for his wallet and retrieving a tattered picture to show Nathan.

"Ooo, tell me that is not me!" Nate chuckles.

"Oh yes, that is you."

"I was an ugly baby."

"No you were not. You were handsome then and you are even more handsome now."

"You don't have to be nice, dad. That's an ugly picture. The fact that you were willing to carry it around tells me I really do mean a lot to you," laughs Nathan, handing the photo back to his father face down.

"You really do mean a lot to me, more than I'll ever be able to tell you and more than you'll ever know. I love you Nathan."

"I love you too, dad. Now let's get some sleep because I want to kick their butts when we go fishing tomorrow."

"Goodnight," replies his father, turning off the lamp. And for the very first time since before Nathan was born and when Abigail and Ola Mae were still alive, Nathaniel sleeps peacefully because he is complete with his Sidekick at his feet.

The following morning, Eva the Grandma Diva was up before the sunrise, preparing a breakfast to remember. It was no secret she felt a good meal was food for the soul. Good eating made people merry and she was always quoting Proverbs 17:22 'A merry heart doeth good like medicine but a broken spirit drieth the bones.'

In her day, Eva had seen more than her share of broken spirits. An even more powerful testimony to the power of happiness to heal a broken spirit was all the people she'd seen restored, emotionally. Starting with her husband, Charles, the list also included Mary and Suzann, Ola Mae, Nathan and she knew in just a matter of time, Nathaniel.

"Good morning," she declares, sliding a cup of coffee to the half-sleep Nathaniel.

"Good morning, Mrs. Eva."

"Mrs. Eva? That's way too formal. Just call me Mama Andrews."

"Can do," replies Nathaniel, taking a sip of the coffee, not bothering to add sugar or cream.

"Nathan, Sweetheart, run and go tell those sleepyheads upstairs to rise and shine. Breakfast is getting cold."

"Yes ma'am."

"He's a good boy. He's come a long way," she says, wiping her hands on an apron and turning her attention to Nathaniel. "How'd you sleep last night?"

The middle-aged man gently places the coffee mug on the counter top. "Peacefully," he sighs.

"I bet you did. Feels good when you realize you are surrounded by love, unconditional forgiving love."

"You're a wise woman, Mama Andrews."

"Hey, what can I say, Hon? With age comes wisdom and stunning beauty," she jokes, stroking her white-gray, feathered Bob.

"You are equally as beautiful, inside and out."

"And you said I'm wise," Eva giggles.

Nathaniel becomes very serious, "Thank you so much for picking up where my mama left off."

"It takes a village, baby, it takes a village," Eva replies, referring to the old African proverb, 'It takes a village to raise a child.'

"Well I'm happy to be inducted into this village," Nathaniel announces proudly.

"Don't ever forget where you came from though. Before you leave Georgia, make it your business to go by the cemetery and visit Ola Mae. It'll do you and Nate both some good."

"I was unsure about going until this very moment. But I give you my word I will do just that."

"Your word is your bond. You can stand on it when you have nothing else."

"Trust me I know," declares Nathaniel in a daze.

"You know what?" butts in Maxwell, entering the kitchen with Mary, Max and Nathan trailing close behind them. "*I'm* going to catch the biggest fish?"

"Don't pay him any attention, Nathaniel. Maxwell is so competitive he still brags about beating our twelve year old son by two measly points in a basketball game."

"Two points or twenty points, that doesn't matter. A win is a win. If I got skills, I got skills. I can't help it the scoreboard spoke volumes."

Everyone laughs as Dr. Andrews struts around the kitchen like a proud peacock, George Jefferson style.

"Sit down and eat, Maxwell!"

"What time 'til we leave for Uncle Al's?" asks Nathan.

"As soon as we eat breakfast and get dressed," exclaims Max.

"I hope we are not getting in a boat," states Nathaniel, rubbing his bulging stomach. "I may sink it, this food is so delicious."

"Do not encourage Mama," chuckles Maxwell. "Every time she visits I gain at *least* four pounds."

"What exactly are you trying to say, Darling Husband?" inquires Mary, putting her hands on her hips. "You wouldn't by any chance be implying I *can't* cook, would you?"

"I would never say that. I just mean you cook healthy, well balanced meals." Maxwell replies, opening the door for Eva to pounce.

"Now it sounds like you are saying your dear ol' mama . . . the woman who spent thirteen agonizing hours bringing you into this world, literally cooks *killer* meals. You wouldn't be saying my cooking is unhealthy and artery clogging would you, Doc?"

"Heavens no, Ma." Maxwell Andrews retreats and kisses Eva on the cheek. "I love you."

"I love you too, son. Now please sit down, take your foot out of your mouth and fill it with food before that ditch you're digging gets any deeper."

Maxwell smirks but recoils. He likes eating like a king and will not risk kidding his way out of a good meal.

"You are truly a diva, Mama Andrews," chuckles Nathaniel.

"And you better know it!" she sasses.

Almost three hours later, the father and son pairs arrive at the home of Al, Suzann and Olivia. The property is enormous and surrounded by large pecan trees.

"This is a nice place you have here," Nathaniel tells Al.

"It's not much, but we call it home."

"It's tranquil."

"If you think this is serene wait until we get down to the pond," comments Maxwell.

"Are ya'lls going to talk all day or is we going fishy?" declares Olivia, tugging at Al's jeans.

"We are going fishing, sweetheart. Run and tell your mommy to give you your life jacket."

"She doesn't have to tell me anything. I have it right here. In fact, here's one for you and you too," Suzann says, tossing Max and Nathan a life preserver as well.

"Thanks," the boys shout, putting them on.

"You're quite welcome," she replies, helping Olivia into her life jacket.

"I'ma catch the biggest fishy in the pond, Mommy. And I want you to give it a bath and cook it with cheese grits."

"You know what I think?" Suzann asks her daughter.

Olivia shakes her curly locks no.

"I think it will be nice if daddy gave your fishy a bath and cooked it with cheese grits. What do you think?"

"I think that's a gooder idea," Olivia says, her eyes lit up like a candlewick. "Daddy, you can wear the Johns Deere ape'ron I got you for Christmas."

Al, Nathaniel, Maxwell, Max and Nathan laugh heartily.

"I'm going to lay it out for Daddy right now," Suzann tells Olivia, tweaking her button nose. "As for you guys, you better get cracking. Mary and Mama Andrews are coming over in a few hours and we want a big mess of fish. And I don't mean from Captain D's either."

"Well gentlemen, and little lady, our mission has been laid before us. Let's show those skeptical women folk what we are made of. Fish beware!" proclaims Al, leading his troops toward his old pick up truck.

"You don't have all day, fellows," Suzann cries out after them. "Mama Andrews has to get on the road in time to make her Bingo game!"

Maxwell was right. The nearly lake-size pond several hundred yards from the Gaffney home was very serene. The ripples created by the gentle breeze could rock a colicky baby to sleep. At that point, Nathaniel didn't care if he catches a single fish. The atmosphere alone was reward enough. Al gave Nathaniel and Nathan a crash course in fishing before the teams paired off.

"What are we fishing for? What kind of fish are in the pond?" asks Nathaniel curiously.

"There's bass, white perch, catfish, you name it and it's likely we'll catch it. Now let the fish-off begin!" shouts Al.

"We got 'dis in the bag, daddy," brags little Olivia.

"Hey, don't count us out," interjects Max. "Me and Dad are about to catch 'em like we are using nets!"

"You tell 'em, son."

"Well, Nathan it looks like we beginners better perfect our fish tales," declares Nathaniel.

"Don't worry, Nate. You are bound to catch something," assures Max.

"Yeah, a bad case of hay fever," laughs Nathan.

The fish are biting and all teams are reeling them in left and right. "Looks like this is turning into a real competition," Nathaniel tells Nate, casting his line again.

"Fishing is fun. I can't believe I'm good at it."

"I can, son. You can be good at anything you put your mind to."

"Do you really believe that?" Nathan asks skeptically. "I've never really been good at anything besides getting into trouble."

"We've all gotten into trouble from time to time. We just have to make a conscience decision to stay out of trouble."

"Dad, you make it sound so easy."

"Nah, Nathan. I'm not saying it's easy, but it gets easier the more you do it. And don't worry. I will help you. Together we can overcome anything, Faithful Sidekick," says Nathaniel, doing his best super hero impression.

"I got another one," yells Nate, struggling to pull this fish onto the bank. "A big one!"

Nathaniel seizes the small opportunity to make good on his promise and aids his son in reeling in the catch of the day. Once they have the fish secure in the bucket with the rest, Nathan notices Al waving them in.

"Suzann is blowing up my cell. Mary and Eva have arrived and they are waiting for us," he hollers.

The teams met at Al's rusty old pick up to tally their catch. Everyone had caught plenty of fish, including the newcomers to the sport, Nate and Nathaniel. The men compare the amount of fish caught and their size. To their amazement Nathan had caught the biggest fish and therefore earned the all-important bragging rights.

"The fish felt sorry for you," jokes Max, "They knew you were leaving and wanted you to have something to boast about in the big city."

"Awe Max-a-million, jealousy is such an ugly color on you," snickers Nate.

"Saddle up men and little lady, we have hungry women to feed," declares Maxwell.

"Maybe we can talk them into helping us clean the fish," hopes Al.

"Yeah and maybe these fish are going to fry themselves," replies Maxwell.

"You can't blame the man for trying," laughs Nathaniel.

Back at the Gaffney residence, Suzann, Mary, and Eva relax in a large redwood stained bench swing. They all rise at the sight of the pick-up approaching.

"It's about time you guys decided to show up. I was about to order me a pizza," winked Eva to her counterparts.

"You know our motto, Mama. Better late than never," teased Maxwell.

"The devil is a liar. Your motto doesn't apply when Bingo is hanging in the balance."

"Well I take it you ladies will be helping us clean the fish then. For the sake of time that is," hints Al.

"Sweetie, take that to the bank and see if you can cash it," giggles Suzann.

"Mommy, Nate catched the biggest fishy but I caught the mostest."

"Good job, Olivia. You have represented us women well," compliments Mary.

"Come on, let's go in the house and get you freshened up," Eva says, escorting Olivia inside.

"Your John Deere apron awaits, Husband," says Suzann.

"And I just so happened to bring your 'World's Greatest Dad' apron, and I even managed to scrape up an extra one for you, too, Nathaniel," adds Mary.

"I guess this means we are off the hook," declares Nate. "We don't have aprons."

"Can we go skip rocks?" asks Max.

"Ask your fathers," Mary replies, going into the house.

Both boys glare at Maxwell and Nathaniel with pleading eyes. "It's fine with me, if it's fine with you," says Nathaniel, placing the burden of making the decision solely on the shoulders of Maxwell.

"Life jackets *must* stay on at all times!"

"Cool!" They gather the preservers from the bed of Al's truck.

"Be back by 3 p.m."

"Okay," they reply, wrestling the life jackets on.

"Don't make us have to come get you."

"I'm going to miss you a lot," confesses Nathan, trying without success to skip a rock clear across the pond.

"It's not going to be peaches and cream around here without you either," admits Max.

"You'll be okay without me. You're a nice person. You ain't going to have a hard time making new friends."

"Not true," interrupts Max. "Look at how we became friends . . . by first being foes. Before you, my only friend was Lucy and before Lucy, my only friend was Granny."

"I had forgotten about that. But still it will be easier for you than me," insists Nathan.

"I'm still going to have to disagree with you," proclaims Max, picking up a medium sized rock and brushing loose debris from it. "You have newness on your side. You'll be in a new place where no one knows you or your past. You can have a fresh wrinkle-free start. *That* gives you the upper hand."

"Whatever. I know I'm going to be trying to get back here as much as I can. I hope we stay as close as we are now."

"There's nothing that can break up our friendship . . . our brotherhood. Not even distance," says Max confidently.

"I hope you are right."

"As Granny would say, '*have I steered you wrong yet?*'" mimics Max.

Both boys chuckle and sink rocks, neither good at skipping stones. Promptly at 3 p.m. the duo trudges back to the home-front.

"You two are right on time. Mary and Suzann are preparing the picnic table to serve dinner. Go wash up using the hose by the driveway," instructs Eva.

"It smells good," says Nate, as they take their places at the table.

"Yeah it smells good. But we better ask a special blessing for this meal, knowing those who prepared it," snickers Suzann, passing out plastic silverware.

"Oh don't front, Girl. You know I can cook. I have you licking your fingers every time I make a meal," defends Al.

Suzann giggles giddily and kisses Al on the cheek, "You know I was just teasing. You are a great cook."

"Allow me to be the judge of that," interjects Eva, the Grandma Diva. "Give me one of those catfish."

Al uses some tongs to place a crispy fried catfish on Eva's plate and anxiously awaits her opinion.

"Lord, bless this fish and the one who caught it. May it nourish my body and not harm it. Amen," taunts Eva, taking a bite of fish.

Everyone quietly waits for her reaction.

"That's pretty good," she mutters, taking another bite. "I'ma have to take a few pieces of that home with me."

"Ha, Suzann! See, I have earned Mama Andrews' expert stamp of approval."

"Oh get over yourself and serve the rest of our guests."

"What guest? We are all family. They better get in where they fit in," laughs Al.

As they eat, Nathaniel marvels at the people he's surrounded by. The Andrews and Gaffney's are the living definition of family. They are a unit, strong and loving, happy and humorous. Each member possesses a characteristic essential to the success of the group as a whole, and in spite of their flaws they are indeed family. The family he's dreamed he, Nathan, Abigail and Ola Mae would be. But fate has other plans for his family and now he had to play the cards life dealt him to the best of his ability.

"What's wrong, Nathaniel," inquires Mary.

"Is your fish alright?" asks Suzann.

"Oh, yeah it's tasty. I was just reminiscing."

"There's nothing like a trip down memory lane to put our current situation in perspective," says Eva.

"You are so right," agrees Al. "Take me for example. A year ago I was a boring bachelor. I lived to work and worked to live, and now look at me. I no longer just exist. I'm a husband, father, friend and world renowned cook."

"What you are is an exaggerator," smirks Suzann. "Your food is edible. I'll even go as far as saying it's savory. But you are a long way from world renowned." She turns her attention to Nathaniel. "The point I think my husband was trying to make is family makes life worth living. Its' the spice of life."

"That's right," adds Mary. "And I personally have learned it's not the number of people in your family that counts. It's each family member making their existence count that's important."

"I really like the way you put that," declares Nathaniel.

"Don't be impressed, Nathaniel," interjects Maxwell. "She's an author. She gets paid to word play."

"Oh, if you keep on, I got some word play for you, Dr. Andrews."

"Son, you better slow your roll before you end up in the doghouse. Mama can't get you out of that one," chuckles Eva.

"I heard that," exclaims Suzann. "Al, take heed."

"See Nathaniel," says Eva, getting serious. "Family is all about faith and fun. And as you can tell, we have that in abundance around here. Our joke cup runneth over."

"I love that about ya'll. You don't just live life, you enjoy it."

"You might as well. You only get one life to live. Instead of being depressed and down, it's best to find something good in every situation and person. Who knows what tomorrow may bring," states Maxwell profoundly.

"I think I'll adopt that as my motto. Find something good in every person and situation," confesses Nathaniel.

"Don't let that go to your head, Maxwell. You are no philosopher," snickers Mary.

"Don't hate, baby. We both know I'm a man of many talents: medicine, basketball, fishing, cooking, master theorist . . . the list is endless."

"More like your imagination is limitless," jabs Mary, causing everyone to laugh.

"I hate to eat and run but it's time I be on my way. If I don't get to the Bingo hall early, Ella-Bell Shavers tries to sit in my spot."

"That's right Granny, you defend your throne and title," instigates Max.

"Come on, Bingo Queen. Allow me to walk you to your chariot," cracks Maxwell.

The others bid Eva farewell. "It's been a pleasure meeting you, Mama Andrews," says Nathaniel.

"Don't you be a stranger," she replies, hugging him tight.

"I'm going to miss you a lot, Granny Eva," professes Nathan, teary eyed.

"No you won't. We'll see each other again before you know it."

"You mean it?"

"Of course I do. Me and Max have always wanted to travel north. I have a brother in Jersey named Gilbert and he's been trying for years to get me up that way. Now I have three reasons to burn up the interstate . . . my brother, you and your daddy."

"Cool!" exclaims Max and Nate excitedly.

"We will be looking forward to your visit," says Nathaniel.

The next couple of days, Nathaniel subtly took a backseat to the Andrews family, allowing Nathan to spend as much time a possible with them. He knew he had the rest of his life to be with Nathan. Slowly they would build the father-son relationship they were supposed to have had years ago. He wanted to be his son's best friend, first confidant, biggest supporter . . . he wanted to evolve into the father portrayed in sitcoms.

Late Thursday afternoon, Nathan showed his father where Ola Mae was buried. As he led his father to his grandmother's grave, Nate fought off silent tears. He refused to breakdown for he thought Nathaniel would need moral support. Ola Mae had always told Nathan he was older than his age and he was starting to understand what she meant. Instead of balling like a fragile little boy, Nathan vowed to let his dad grieve for Ola Mae.

"Dad, I'm going to give you a few minutes to talk to Me'ma alone," Nate announces, backing up to give Nathaniel some privacy.

Nathaniel lays fresh long stemmed pink roses on his mother's headstone and begins to sob.

Nathan's heart ached for his father. He couldn't imagine what he was going through. Yes, Ola Mae had raised Nathan and played the motherly role, yet she was still just his grandmother. True enough his own mother was also deceased but he had never had the privilege of actually knowing her. It's hard to truly miss for someone you never knew personally. He could only grieve what he *thought* having his mother would be like. But Nathaniel, on the other hand, had known Ola Mae. He'd grown up under her wing. Even after a long separation, losing her had to be extremely hard.

When Nate sees Nathaniel kneel down, he becomes overcome by emotion. His Sidekick instincts activate and he hurries to his hero's aid.

"I'm here for you, dad," he says, cupping Nathaniel's head to his thin chest. "Me'ma understands. She's not mad. She loved you. She forgave you, remember?"

As Nathan's words sink in, Nathaniel begins to pull himself together. Nate was right. Ola Mae was a kind, very understanding soul, so quick to forgive and so slow to anger.

"Thank you, Nathan."

"That's what sidekicks are for."

"Well, trusty Sidekick, I hope you are ready to take on New York tomorrow."

"Let the adventure begin!"

Nathaniel smiles, "Let's venture towards to the Andrews' house. The sun is going down and we have to get up kind of early in the morning. Plus, something tells me you and Max want to play video games together one last time."

Nathaniel and Nathan hop in the rental car and head back. "Don't be too sad, dad. We are taking Me'ma with us in our hearts. That's where I have been carrying her since she passed. She *is* my heart. All the good in me and love in me she put there. All of that keeps me going just like the heart keeps the body going."

"Oh son, she was with me the whole time I was gone, tucked safely within me, too. All of you were, your mother, grandmother and you."

"You know what?" asks Nate, staring blankly at the car's interior roof.

"What, Sidekick?"

"We are going to take the Andrews to New York with us in our hearts, too."

"Right you are, Nathan, right you are."

As they pull into the driveway fifteen minutes later, Nate's heart sinks.

"All the lights are off. You don't think they have gone to bed already do you, dad?"

"Can't really say one way or the other, son," Nathaniel replies honestly. "Maxwell, Mary, and Max have all been going to tremendous efforts to keep us entertained these past couple days. It wouldn't surprise me if they are exhausted."

"Awe," groans Nate, obviously disappointed.

"Don't worry Nathan. If they are asleep, I'm sure you and Max will be able to squeeze in at least one quick video game before we leave for the airport."

"Okay."

"Now quiet," Nathaniel cautions Nathan as they step up onto the porch of the Andrews home. He retrieves the extra key from under a potted plant. "If they are sleeping, I don't want to wake them."

Fumbling, Nathaniel manages to unlock and open the front door. Nathan flips the living room light switch.

"Surprise!" a crowd yells.

Everyone who ever meant anything to Nathan is there: Principal Hill, he and Ola Mae's former neighbor, Ms. Shirley, Jerome "Big Mac" MacAuthur, his parents and siblings, the Gaffney's, Eva the Grandma Diva, and of course the Andrews themselves, including the canine family members, Sam and Lucky. His eyes gloss over in emotion. Balloons, streamers, and flashing disco lights provide an explosion of color throughout and there is a huge banner draped from one end of the room to the other stating 'We'll miss you Nate the Great!'

"Ya'll really care about me. No one has ever had a party for me. Nobody would have bothered to come!"

"We'll this party is all about you!" yells Max over all the partygoers banter.

"Pump up the music," demands Eva. "Come on Nathan, let's cut some rug."

The going away party lasts late into the night. Everyone has a blast dancing, eating and sharing Nate the Great stories. When the festivities are over and the guests say their final farewells, Nathan is blessed with many going away gifts. Once the last guest is gone, he joins his father in the Andrews spare bedroom.

"Dad, that beat the heck out of videos! Didn't it?"

"I don't believe they have created a video game that can hold a candle to that party," agrees Nathaniel.

"If you don't mind, I want to spend my last night here with Max in our room. We are going to talk and play with Sam and Lucky until morning or until Granny Eva comes and makes us go to sleep."

"I don't mind at all, Sidekick. I understand."

"Thanks Superhero."

"Love you."

"I love you, too."

"Knock, knock," says Nate, entering the room he and Max would no longer share.

"What's up?" asks Max, tossing off his sheet and sitting up.

"Nothing. You wasn't sleeping, was you?"

"Nah, I can't really sleep. I'm too wound up."

"I know the feeling," replies Nathan.

"I figured you would be spending the night talking to your father, like you have every night since he came back," Max whines, a little bitter with jealousy.

"Dad and I will have plenty of time to talk once we get to New York and get settled in. Me, Sam, and Lucky thought we'd spend my last night with my other best friend. That is if you don't mind."

Max lights up with cheer. "What are you waiting for time is ticking away. Get your narrow behind on in here so I can kick it in a game of Madden."

Of course, Eva the Grandma Diva had to check in on them, and watching them through Max's cracked bedroom door, she can't bring herself to bust up the party.

"If you can't beat 'em Eva, join 'em," she tells herself, making her presence known to the two young boys.

"Sorry, Granny, we didn't mean to make so much noise. We just finished our last game," whispers Max, guilt ridden.

"Oh heavens no, child, you didn't wake me. I was just passing by to get a drink of water from the kitchen and saw the light was still on."

"Granny Eva, can you say a bedtime prayer for us?" asks Nathan, knowing Eva's guidance is going to be one of the things he'll miss the most.

"I sure can," she declares, getting down on her knees and clutching both of the boys' hands.

"Make this one special, Granny. One that me and Nate can say each night to keep us connected."

"I think I can handle that," Eva replies, summoning her creativity. The bedroom grows quiet and Max and Nathan wait for Eva to speak.

"Dear Lord, thank You for gracing us to live to see another day. Thank You for loving us and guiding our way. Thank You for kind words to say. Forgive us our sins we honestly pray and bless our family from New York to G–A Amen."

"Amen," the boys chant together.

"That was poetic, Granny. Dr. Seuss ain't got nothing on you," chuckles Max.

"Yeah, Granny Eva, you got your religious rap on. That's going to be easy for me to remember. Me and Max can say that prayer every night at 9:30 p.m. so we can still be connected."

"Every night at 9:30 p.m." concurs Max, liking the idea of still being in touch with Nathan spiritually, for it has become their custom to say their prayers together.

"Help me to my feet and follow me to my room. I have something I want to show you," declares Eva.

Max and Nate tiptoe on Eva's heels to her room.

"Gently shut the door and climb up here on Granny's bed while I find my glasses."

They comply, leaving the middle of the bed vacant for Eva to sit between them.

"Check this out," she proclaims, taking her place in the middle.

"What is it?" asks Max, admiring the leathery cover of the book.

"It's kind of like a baby book for Nathan."

"A baby book?" repeats Nate, puzzled. "How can you have a baby book for me? You didn't know me when I was a baby."

"Well, I hadn't thought about it quite like that. So I guess for arguments sake we better call it a scrap book."

"Come on, Granny, open it up. We want to know what you have stuck in there," insists Max impatiently.

"We are going to work on your patience, *my* Max," she says, opening the album to reveal it's first images.

The very first picture on the page is identical to the picture Nathaniel had shown Nathan, except it was a 5x7.

"Oh no!" sighs Nate, embarrassed. "Not the ugly baby picture."

"It's not ugly, Hon, it's nice. Look at the head full of hair you had," Eva tells Nathan, pointing.

"Where did you get that from, Granny," inquires Max.

"I found this picture along with a few others in Ola Mae's Bible. The landlord where Nate and his grandmother lived was going to trash all the things left behind. And you know your Granny was not about to let anybody throw away a copy of the Word."

"I never knew she had these."

"Well they are yours to cherish now and forever Nathan. Consider this my gift to you and your dad. I gift wrapped Ola Mae's tattered Bible and gave it to your dad earlier when the presents were exchanged. He said he ain't going to open it until ya'll get to New York."

"I'll act surprised when he opens it."

The scrapbook Eva the Grandma Diva made included the newborn picture of Nathan, a Polaroid of Nathaniel as a child, Nathan's parents wedding picture, a faded snap shot of a younger Ola Mae and a handsome stranger with strong features, and a cut-out of the headline featuring Nathan's fiasco at Johnston County Middle school, all collected from the Bible. Ola Mae kept the good and the bad. Eva had also inserted pictures of Nathan at Andrews' family gatherings. Nate was glad Eva has captured the best Christmas of his life on film. She even threw in a few pictures of the puppies, Sam and Lucky. Taped to the back inside cover was a copy of Ola Mae's obituary.

"As you see, there ain't many pictures in here. I was going to fill them as time passed. Now I'm passing on that task to you and your daddy. When Max and me come to visit you, I expect to see some new additions. You hear me?" she says, embracing Nathan.

"Yes ma'am. You have my word and my word is my bond," he states softly but stern, as he rubs his fingertips across the image of his mother, amazed. It is the first time he's ever seen her.

"Document your past as a reminder. That way you'll be less likely to repeat the bad and you'll be able to draw encouragement and strength from the good."

Eva was pleased the message of her late husband had successfully been passed on to four young black men: Maxwell, Max, Nathaniel and Nathan. Charles couldn't express enough the value of an honest man's word. He felt the new generation of African American men's shameless lack of self-respect had led to the blatant growth of their disrespect . . . disrespect for their heritage, their queens, and their offspring.

"You can't love anybody else if you don't first love yourself. Same goes with respect," Charles often said. *"Man is supposed to love the Lawd with all his heart. Love his neighbor as himself and love his wife as Christ loved the church. We gotta get back to that and we are going to start with Maxwell Andrews."* He had indeed effectively instilled those things in their son.

CHAPTER TWO

Tourist Sites & Big City Lights

Nathan had never flown before; in fact he had never been outside of Doversville that he could remember. Although he was a little fearful, curiosity took the cake. Watching all the large aircrafts take off and land through a huge plate glass window made him even more anxious. However, Nate's growing curiosity and anxiety was going to have to play second fiddle to patience. The voice bellowing from the intercom broadcasted the Campbell's flight had been substantially delayed because of thick fog.

"Are you hungry, son?"

"Not really. But if you are, I'll eat something," says Nathan.

They sit several more minutes in the terminal without chatting. Nathaniel could hear the rumble in his son's stomach over the airport noise and was trying to figure out why Nathan said he wasn't really hungry.

"Nathan, you're hungry. I hear your stomach growling. Why would you say 'not really' when I asked?"

Nate stares at the lightly littered coffee colored airport floor. "Me and Me'ma never really had enough money to eat out. We had to pinch every penny to make ends meet. And I know these plane tickets wasn't cheap and I didn't want to make you spend any more money."

Guilt for abandoning his son once again hits Nathaniel like a two-ton boulder. "Look at me, son," he says, turning Nathan's humiliated face towards his own. "Don't worry about spending. That's why I make money. To spend it. To spend it on you and try to make your life better. Now don't get me wrong, we are not rich. But we do pretty good and in due time we'll be doing even better. Until then, I believe buying a couple of burgers won't send us to the soup kitchen."

"Sorry," Nathan apologizes.

"For what, Nate? You should never be sorry for being honest about how you feel and what you've been through or may be going through. I'm the one who is sorry . . . sorry I wasn't there to help you and Mama. I wanted to. I really did. I hope you believe that. Back then, I couldn't even help myself though."

"If I can get a deluxe bacon cheeseburger, we'll call it even!"

"That sounds delicious. I think we'll both get one," smiles Nathaniel.

Inside one of the airport's deli-style restaurants, they order deluxe bacon cheeseburgers, fries, one chocolate and one strawberry milkshake. Nathan uses the wait to show is father the scrapbook Eva has started.

"Mom was so good-looking," he says, outlining his mothers face on the photograph.

"She had natural beauty. I can't ever remember your mother wearing not even a dab of make-up. Lotion and chap stick were the extent of her beauty regimen," Nathaniel states profoundly, recalling the exquisite woman who once adorned his arm.

"Tell me about her?" Nathan says cautiously, tapping his foot on the checkerboard title floor.

His father takes a deep breath. "What would you like to know? Where do you want me to begin?"

"Begin at the beginning, start with how you two met."

Nathaniel sits back in the brick-red booth and folds his arms across his chest. "Abigail and I met on the shoulder of the road."

"On the side of the road? You mean my mama was a . . . a . . . hook . . ."

"Hitchhiker," laughs Nathaniel. "She had car trouble. Listen, let me explain: Me and my friends were walking to work and came across your mother stranded on the side of the road. Her car had broken down and she was in a panic. Not because of the car, but because she didn't want her father worrying himself sick about her being late getting home."

"Sounds like Mama was real thoughtful."

"She was. Her mannerisms were a lot like your Me'ma's."

"Wow, that's why you liked her, huh?"

"Yeah, I have to say that was one of the many reasons why I liked her."

"Okay, finish the story. So you were a superhero that day, too, and saved Princess Abigail, damsel in distress, right?" asks Nate, liking the fairy tale direction he feels his father's story was headed.

"Kind of. Honestly Nathan, your old man wasn't much of a mechanic, but your grandpa Campbell was. I sent my friends ahead to call him to come help, while I stayed behind to wait with Abigail."

Nathaniel lit up for no apparent reason. Thus far in his story, Nate hadn't found anything funny . . . warm but not funny.

"Dad, why are you smiling?"

"I can't help it, son. I can still see your mother pacing the side of the highway. Beads of sweat causing her face to spark when the bright sunshine hit 'em. She had on an orange sundress. Orange was her favorite color. Her hair was pulled back in a ponytail and she had on flip-flops with metal quarter sized flat seashells across the straps of them. The more she trampled the grass wearing it down in concern, not for herself but her ailing father, the more I knew she was the one for me.

However, for your mother it wasn't love at first sight. I had to grow on her. Back then I was quite rough around the edges. Your mother's father always referred to me as *the hood up to no good*."

"Were you a thug, dad?"

Nathaniel thinks hard before answering the question. "I would have never considered myself a thug or a hood. I like to think I was beyond misunderstood. I had goals but I didn't exactly go about achieving them the right way. Funny thing was, your mother and me, we shared the same goal. She was patient and knew that in time her persistence would pay off. Me, on the other hand, I wanted instant results for my labor. But Abigail Jackson saw passed all that. She had faith that I would get it right."

"What was the goal you and Mama shared?" inquires Nathan, hanging on Nathaniel's every word.

"We wanted to own a salon/barber shop. Doing hair was your mama's passion. It made her happy to make people feel good about themselves and the way they looked, and I was fierce with a pair of clippers. But see, your mother was willing to go the extra yard and go to beauty school. Not me though. I wanted to cut hair right then, but since I wasn't a licensed barber I couldn't own a business. Which is understandable now, but back then it only frustrated me. I wanted the business without the backing is what your Me'ma used to say when I whined to her."

"Here you are," says a very tall waitress with fiery red hair, placing an identical plate down in front of each of them. "Now which one of you gentlemen had the chocolate shake and which one had the strawberry?'

"Strawberry right here," replies Nathan, raising his hand.

"Well I guess that means Dad gets the chocolate," declares the waitress, handing the large cup to Nathaniel.

"Thank you."

"You're quite welcome, sugar, and if ya'll need anything else just holler. My name is Jessie."

"Thank you again," says Nathaniel as she walks away.

"Back to the you and Mama. What happened next? Did she go to beauty school?"

"Yeah, she went to beauty school after we were married. Your Grandpa Jackson was furious. He didn't want your mother to marry me. He said he didn't know what she saw in me. I admit, at times I wondered myself what your mother saw in me.

We moved into this tiny little apartment not far from where your Me'ma lived. I worked two part-time jobs while your mom went to school. Once she finished school and got hired on at a salon, we would have enough income for me to quit one of my part-time jobs and it would be my turn to go to school. But things didn't quite work out that way.

Soon after we moved into our small apartment, we found out you were on your way. Your mother *did* get to finish school before you were born and she passed away. But that, of course, was as far as our dreams got. Without Abigail I was lost. I didn't know my rooter from my tooter. I had to get away," Nathaniel concludes, pain cracking his voice.

"Can I ask you something . . . something that I've been wondering about every since I was old enough to understand what happened to my mama."

His father takes a swish of his shake and nods.

"Did you leave me because I killed Mama?"

Nathaniel looks horrified. "Nathan, no, you didn't kill your mother. It was not your fault and I never want you to think it was. Your mother had a weak heart and none of us knew it. Not even her. Guilt was part of the reason I left. I felt like in some kind of way I should have known. I thought you would hate me for not being able to save your mother. Your Grandpa Jackson hated himself too. He felt he, of all people, should have known something was wrong with *his* daughter. We have never spoken since the day you were born, not even at your mother's funeral.

Guilt has been eating away at us all, but I realized not long ago Nathan we all loved Abigail and she loved us. Including you Nathan, your mother loved you and had big dreams for you. And I know with every ounce of my being that she wouldn't want us bickering and blaming ourselves. She'd want our love for her and her love for us to be enough to bind us forever."

Nate absorbs his father's words. "Can I ask you something else?"

"Sure, what is it?"

"Where is my mama buried? After Me'ma's funeral, I searched the whole cemetery twice for a headstone with my mama's name on it, but I never found one."

"Your mother is buried in your Grandpa Jackson's back yard under a large shady oak tree. The same tree she used to sit under on a blanket as a little girl and read. Even though we were married and I had the last so-say in where she would be laid to rest, I thought it was only right to allow your grandpa to bury her there. After all, I'd have a piece of her close to me forever . . . you. I let your grandfather have your mother's remains close to him so he could visit her when he wanted to."

"That was a nice thing to do for a man who never liked you," remarks Nate.

"Yeah well, just because your grandfather didn't like me, that doesn't mean I felt the same way about him. I admired Willie Jackson. I respected him for serving our country, going to war, losing his leg and never complaining. He always spoke of his military days with such pride. But most of all I held him in the highest regard because without him there would have been no Abigail Jackson-Campbell. Anyhow there will be plenty of time to talk more about that later.

Right now you need to eat your food because they only serve a little pack of peanuts and a soda on the plane."

"Okay."

Nathaniel and Nathan consume their meals and chat idly for a good forty-five minutes before the boarding call for their flight is announced.

"I'm a little bit scared," admits Nate.

"Don't worry Nathan, there's nothing to flying. And you're lucky. Since it will be night when we arrive, you'll see all the big city lights. New York at its finest, illuminated and luxurious."

"I can hardly wait!"

On the plane Nathan listened attentively as the attendant gave the flight instructions. Nathaniel, who had flown a few times before, fastened his seat belt and began to thumb through a magazine. Nate was very mindful of the instructions and repeated them several times to himself.

"Would you like a pair of wings?" asks one of the flight attendants while checking to see if Nathan's seat belt was fastened correctly.

"Can I have two so I can send one to my best friend in Doversville?"

"I think that can be arranged," she says, winking. "I'll bring them to you after takeoff."

"Thanks," he says, turning his attention to his surroundings. "Dad, this is like being in a long movie theater without the movie."

Nathan was right. The rows of blue cloth padded seats and the aisles down the middle really did mimic a theater setting. And just like the movies, the flight had attendants, too.

"Believe it or not, son, some planes do show a movie during the flight."

"Really?" Nate inquires, not believing his ears.

"Really!" Nathaniel laughs.

When the plane's engine began to roar Nathan's heart pounds. *"This is it,"* he thinks.

"Don't worry, son, it's going to be just fine. The takeoff and landing is the rockiest parts of flying." Nathaniel conveniently omits possible turbulence.

Although Nate had exaggerated the occurrence in his mind,

slightly hoping he would experience being pinned back to his seat with galactic Star Wars force, Nathaniel was right. As the plane took off, Nathan felt only a slight shift of his insides. The same shifting feeling he'd often experienced in elevators, just in a different direction. And as their altitude increased, his ears popped, leaving Nathan feeling like they are filled with water. Well, more like he felt when he'd blown his nose too long and hard, because his hearing was muffled.

"Here Nathan," declares Nathaniel, "This gum will help the crazy feeling in your ears."

"I hope so. I feel weird."

"I promise it will go away eventually."

As Nathaniel promised, the bizarre feeling did go away. The flight attendant gave Nathan two pairs of wings as well. He puts them, along with one of the pack of peanuts, in his pants pocket. He planned to send the salty snack to Max, too.

"You might as well enjoy the total flying experience," says Nathaniel lifting the window shade and exposing the shrinking world below.

Without uttering a word or breaking his gaze out the window, Nate managed to maneuver a set of headphones out of his pocket. However, he never bobbed his head or tapped his toes to any beat. The darker it got, the deeper he peered at the growing number of twinkles below.

"Are you okay?"

"Yes sir," whispers Nathan, "It's like the stars fell to the ground."

"I knew you would be mesmerized."

"I feel like I'm in outer space, twinkling stars above me and below me. It reminds me of the movies when the rich people fly on their private planes."

Nathaniel doesn't say anything else. He silently lets Nathan take pleasure in the multitude of man-made lights below them accented by God's sprinkle of glowing glitter above them.

When the plane landed, Nathan was still in a daze. He doesn't remember exiting the craft or retrieving their luggage. In fact he didn't snap back into the real world until the cab ride home.

"Where to?" asks the fat balding cab driver, taking one last drag off a cigarette as they climb into the backseat.

"The Heights," replies Nathaniel, waving the second hand smoke back towards the front of the cab.

"Sorry sir, I'm putting it out now," the cab driver says, smashing the smoldering cigarette butt in the ashtray.

"Thanks for respecting me and my son. A lot of drivers couldn't care less. They see passengers as fares only."

"Oh, no problem. I've been trying to quit for about a month now. And as long as I have customers in here, I'm good. But it's when I'm alone that I can't resist. I smoke for comfort, for companionship," he confesses.

"Well keep the faith. Where there's a will there's a way. Anything worth having is worth the struggle to achieve it and I believe being nicotine free will be worth it in the end. It could very well save your life," declares Nathaniel, sounding a bit like Eva, Ola Mae and the TRUTH commercials.

"Mister, you said a mouthful. "The driver turns the rearview mirror towards Nathan, "You better listen to your dad, young man. Smoking is bad for you and a hard habit to kick. I'm living proof of that."

"I hate smoke," announces Nate. "It stanks and makes everything around it stank, too."

Nathaniel nudged his son, hoping he'd get the hint and exercise a little tact. Spare the cabby's feelings some. After all, the man was trying to quit smoking. He didn't want Nathan giving him a reason to light one up as soon as he puts them out by stressing him. However, the cab driver laughed so hard he started coughing, a harsh raspy hacking.

"I bet he's coughing like that because he smokes," Nate thought to himself. *"Yuk!"*

The ride home was a long one. As they traveled further away from the airport, Nathan noticed a change in the housing conditions. Oddly, it had never occurred to him to ask his father what he did for a living or what kind of apartment he lived in. All he knew about his father's apartment was it has two bedrooms.

"Dad, what do you do? Do you live in the projects?"

Nathaniel massaged the bridge of his nose, knowing the last place Nathan wanted to live was the projects. He'd lived in the projects his whole life up until Ola Mae's passing and his moving into the Andrews' home. Nathaniel understood his son's apprehension. Who would want to move back into the projects after living in a quaint detached family home as nice as the one he's just left, the home he was growing accustomed to.

"I own a barbershop called Clipper Creations. I'm a building super and part-time youth counselor."

Nathan's hope is temporarily restored. If his father owns a business, he can't possibly be living in the projects.

"So your dream did come true."

"Kind of, part of it anyway."

"Mama and Me'ma would be so proud of you."

"I hope so."

"They would, Superhero."

"You know exactly what to say to make your dad feel better, Sidekick."

Nate goes back to street gazing.

"Nathan?" his father says hesitantly.

"Sir?" he replies, not bothering to make eye contact.

"The Heights is income-based housing, *but* it's come a long way. If it hadn't, you would still be in Georgia," Nathaniel professes earnestly.

"Your dad is right. The Heights have come a long way. There was a time, not so long ago, that I would have told you two to get out of my cab because I refused to go to The Heights. But the tenants have began a strong crusade to take back their buildings."

"That's right," nods Nathaniel.

"I commend you all and your efforts, sir. The world would be a better place if people would stop ignoring crime and turning a blind eye to the hardship of their fellow man. If more communities would take a zero tolerance stance, we'd see tremendous results worldwide."

"Amen!" exclaims Nathaniel. "Sounds like you have a little crusader in you, too."

They laugh.

"I do what I can and try to encourage others to do the same."

"Amen again! In order for *each one to teach one*, first *each one must* reach *one*."

"I have to Amen that. You're a lucky young man there . . . ?"

"Nathan Campbell," Nate the Great speaks up.

"You're a lucky young man, Nathan Campbell. Your father is a real descent man."

"I know and it doesn't matter where we live as long as we live *together.*"

"My sentiments exactly."

Approximately fifteen minutes later, the cabby announces they have made it.

The Heights didn't look too bad. The buildings were several stories high, Nate guessed about four. There's a wrought iron fence around the entire group of buildings and appeared to be some kind of neighborhood watch station set up at the entrance and exit of The Heights. In the center of the housing was a large playground. Nothing fancy, just a few metal swing sets, a seesaw, a set of monkey bars, three different sized slides, and a sandbox.

After Nathaniel pays the cab driver, the graying person manning the fenced entrance helps them with their bags.

"It's about time you decided to come back," he laughs, slapping Nathaniel on the back.

"I had some very important business to attend to," replies Nathaniel.

"Oh there's nothing wrong with getting away. A mini vacation would do a lot of us some good. If I could convince Cora to leave New York, I'd like to go on a second honeymoon. It's been 32 years and we have yet to skip a beat," the man, says rolling the largest of the luggage through the gate.

"32 years? That's a blessing, Mr. Dan."

"Who you telling?" chuckles the old man. "It's amazing I've managed to stay with her this long. Don't tell her I said it, but she snores like a cave full of hibernating grizzly bears."

"That tiny little soft spoken woman snores? I can't even imagine."

"Trust me, she's speaks softly because her throat probably hurts all the time from the way she raises the roof."

Nathan can't hold his snicker at the old man's seriousness.

"Oh I'm sorry," declares Nathaniel, realizing he hasn't introduced Nate. "Mr. Dan, this is my son Nathan. Nathan, this is a very special man around here, Mr. Dan."

Mr. Dan stops in his tracks, "Son?"

"Yes sir, my son."

"Well I'm delighted to meet you, Nathan."

"It's nice to meet you, too," Nate replies, shaking the man's hand.

"Whenever you get settled in, you're going to have to come by. I live in apartment 4 and I'll have Cora bake you some goodies or something."

"That sounds good."

"Oh Nathan, you are in for a treat. Mrs. Cora can throw down in the kitchen," confirms Nathaniel.

"I'm going to get back to my security duty and let you two get a goodnight's rest," says Mr. Dan, rolling the bag into building 1's hallway and positioning it in front of a door numbered one. Nathaniel opens the apartment door and instructs Nathan to take all of the bags inside.

"Has everything been okay? There wasn't any trouble while I was gone was it?"

"Nothing me and Sydney couldn't handle. She's a tough little cookie. J-ran and his hoodlum pant-sagging friends tried her when she was on security duty, but she put them in their place fast! She didn't need my help none.

One of J-ran's buddies called her out her name and smacked her on her backside. She grabbed that boy in some kind of choke hold that made me say *Lord have mercy.*"

"I can see Sydney doing something like that. She's a Southern girl and southern girls don't play when it comes to disrespect. Anyhow, I'm glad you two held things down for me while I was away. I'll see you in the morning."

"Okay Nathaniel, you get some rest."

The men part ways, "Hey, Mr. Dan?" Nathaniel calls out after him.

"Yes?"

"Were there any maintenance problems, leaking faucets, clogged toilets, cracked windows? You know what I'm saying, were there any tenant issues?"

"Like I told you, Nathaniel, nothing me and Sydney couldn't handle."

"Thanks, Mr. Dan. Goodnight."
"Night Nathaniel."

That first night in New York Nathan was so tired from traveling he didn't really get a chance to look the place over. He showered, brushed his teeth, said the prayer Eva made up for him and Max before falling fast asleep. Nathaniel spent most of the night unpacking and putting Nathan's things away. He wanted the apartment to reflect his true feelings . . . the feeling that Nathan belonged there. It was *their* apartment . . . *their* home.

The next morning Nathaniel wakes Nate early. "Rise and shine, Nathan. We have to get a jump on things. I have to run by the barbershop to check on a few things. Then we'll try to catch a few tourist sites."

"Great," exclaims Nate, jumping out of bed.

"I put your clothes in the bathroom. As soon as you're dressed, we'll leave," his father announces.

"What about breakfast?" yells Nathan from the bathroom.

"We're going to have breakfast, New York style."

"What does that mean?" Nate asks curiously.

"That means we are going to stop at one of the vendors and grab a couple bagels."

"Oh," sighs Nate, not sure if he liked the way that sounded.

Ten minutes later father and son are headed out of the apartment complex. There was someone else sitting at the gate's security booth.

"Morning Nathaniel," says the very attractive woman. "Mr. Dan told me you were back."

"Good morning, Sydney. Thanks for holding down the fort while I was gone."

"You don't have to thank me. I have to live here just like you. It's my pleasure to do anything I can to keep the building nice and drug free."

"Sydney, I want you to meet a very special young man . . . my son Nathan."

"Wow, it's good to meet you, Nathan," she says, shaking Nate's hand. "You have your father's good looks."

Nathan is taken back by Sydney's compliment. He instantly feels a huge crush growing within him. "You smell really nice and you have really soft hands."

"Oh man, did I just say that out loud," Nate asks himself, embarrassed at his blunder.

"Thanks. My secret is coco butter lotion."

"We'll catch you later, Syd. We have to make a few stops," intervenes Nathaniel.

"See you later, little Nathan."

"Bye, Ms. Sydney," Nate replies with dreamy eyes.

"Put some pep in your step, son. We are going to hump it a few blocks before we hail a cab. My favorite bagel vendor is a couple blocks away."

"Hungry as I am, we can jog if you want to," laughs Nathan.

"How about I meet you half way and we'll just power walk?"

"Deal!"

The few blocks from the apartment building to the vendor are lost in the growing mob of people that litter the streets. Nathan had never seen so many people walking the streets in his life. The sidewalks of Doversville Georgia on their busiest day couldn't hold a candle to those of New York on its lightest days. The hustle and bustle of this new environment was going to take some getting used to.

"Hi Nathaniel," greets the jolly man behind the bagel cart. "Who is that you have with you?"

"Morning, Simon. This is my son Nathan."

"How are you, Nathan?" asks the vendor.

"Hungry," Nate replies bluntly.

"You'll have to excuse him, Simon. Right now he can't seem to think past his stomach," apologizes Nathaniel.

"No need for apologies. I understand completely what the lad is going through. A man's got to eat. Don't you worry. I have just the thing to calm your hunger monster," declares Simon, handing Nathan a huge bagel.

"Thank you, Mr. Simon."

"You are quite welcome." Simon hands Nathaniel a small brown bag and Nathaniel hands Simon some money.

"Keep the change," Nathaniel says, hailing a cab.

The cab ride to Nathaniel's barbershop was short. The name of the shop, Clipper Creations, was sprayed graffiti style on the barbershop's large windows. There was also a red and blue swirling thing attached to the outside wall near the window. Nathan had seen those things many times at the barbershops back home but he didn't know what they were called.

"We could have walked here," comments Nate.

"Yes we could have, but time is precious today," says Nathaniel, holding the door for Nathan to enter the shop.

"What up, Boss Man?" inquires a really young looking man with fancy designs cut into his fade haircut.

"I appreciate you keeping things going while I was in Georgia, Bryan."

"Hey, I gotta eat just like you do, and if I can't cut hair I can't eat either. So I appreciate you allowing me to keep the biz open while you handle your biz."

"Bryan, this is my seed, Nathan," Nathaniel declares, introducing Nate.

Bryan puts down his clippers and walks over to Nate. "Give me some pound, lil' dude," he says, extending his clinched fist.

Nate makes a fist and hits Bryan's with it. "Cool tatts, Mr. Bryan," Nathan replies, admiring the many tattoos covering Bryan's arms. Two really captivated him. One was a bright red apple with a knight's sword driven into it in front of a cluster of skyscrapers, and the other was an antique Cinderella chariot with Charity written on its door.

"You got a good eye there, dude, and you can call me B. All my friends do."

"Okay . . . B."

"Nathan, have a seat. Bryan and I have to discuss something real quick."

"Alright, dad."

Nathaniel and Bryan enter a back room of the barbershop labeled 'Office.' Nathan sat in an empty red cracked leather barber chair and spun around.

"Careful there, Nathan, that chair is money. If it's not functional, it's not producing funds," declares an old dark skinned man with a long white beard holding a straight razor. Except for the cornrows, the man could easily double as Nathan's mental picture of Moses from the Bible.

"Who are you and what are you talking about?" says Nate, ready to give the elderly man a piece of his mind.

"I'm Isaac, the shop manager, and my statement means if you break that chair you are breaking the bank. If we can't use that chair, that's one less head we can cut and less money in the register at the end of the day."

"If you are the manager then why did my dad just thank B for keeping the shop running?" Nathan asks, tittering on disrespect.

"As you can see, I'm not the youngest cat in here. Bryan was the one who opened the shop up every day, but I'm the one who makes sure everything runs like a well oiled machine," Isaac states, returning his focus to the customer he was shaving.

Nathan spins the chair one more time before he takes in the scenery around him. Clipper Creations had a white tile floor and six cutting stations. Each station had a large red barber's chair with a big cushioned gray pad underneath it. There are sinks and endless supplies on the wall-to-wall counter tops. Each station had its own large mirror positioned over its sink. The barbers all wear powder blue hip length lab coats with large pockets. And the parts of the walls that aren't mirrored had pictures of African Americans that Nathan had never seen before.

"How old are you, Nathan?" asks Isaac.

"Twelve. How old are you?" sasses Nate, just as his father is coming out of his office.

"Old enough to tan your hide without my permission," says Nathaniel, putting his son in check.

"Let him be, Nathaniel. He's young, he'll learn," replies Isaac.

"He's about to learn the hard way, Mr. Isaac. I will not put up with him disrespecting you or any other adult. Instead of getting smart with you, he should be sitting down listening to you . . . let you educate him so that he can be smarter than his mouth."

Nathan felt lower than low. He wished he could cower under the barber chair he was in. Quickly he had to get a grip on his tongue. Nemesis Nate the Great was beginning to take over and Nathan couldn't let that happen. Nate the Great was nothing but a great deal of trouble. Trouble could get him sent away . . . trouble could separate him from his father.

"Sorry, Mr. Isaac."

"Apology accepted."

"Come on, Nathan, let's go before your mouthpiece gets you put under house-arrest. There are too many sites to see to get your freedom taken."

"Sorry, dad."

"Don't be sorry, Nathan. Be respectful."

"If I may make a suggestion," interjects Mr. Isaac.

"Sure you can. You know how much I value your opinion," proclaims Nathaniel.

"I suggest you take the boy to Harlem and show him a few things."

"Sounds like the perfect place to start," Nathaniel agrees.

"Can we see the Apollo Theater?" inquires Nate warily.

"We'll see," Nathaniel replies, plainly turning his attention to Bryan and Mr. Isaac, "We'll see you guys tonight at closing."

"A'ight, Boss Man."

"Although I think Sandman is cool, we are not going to the Apollo Theater. I want to go see some real sites, like the Empire State Building or the Statue of Liberty," Nate says to himself and plans to persuade his father.

Nathaniel decided it would be a good idea for them to walk a few blocks before hailing a cab. He was steaming at Nathan for the way he smarted off to Mr. Isaac. If he had learned nothing else from his past experiences, he knew it was wise not to take any type of action while angry. Plus, being this was he and Nate's very first solo day together, he'd walk clear to California before he would ruin or damage their newly forming family foundation.

"Dad, I know you are still mad. I can tell because you have the same look on your face Me'ma used to have when she was mad at me."

Nathaniel half smiles, "I am a little upset."

Nate chews on his bottom lip as he thinks of what to say next. "I'm trying really hard . . . it's real easy to be bad. Going straight takes plenty of work. I have to remind myself to do the right thing even if it doesn't feel good."

"Those are some very wise words for a twelve year old," declares his father, placing his hand on Nathan's shoulder, attempting to lighten the weight of the world upon them.

"Why is it so hard to be good, to be positive?" Nathan asks, earnestly and tormented.

"Well, son, when you really think about it, it's not really that hard to be good. It just takes strength. Stay strong and prayerful. You can find the strength to do anything you need to through prayer. The Bible says *'I can do all things through Christ which strengthens me'* and *'with God all things are possible,'* I'm living proof of those scriptures."

Nathan was very taken back by his father's biblical knowledge. Never in any of his daydreams about him had his dad ever quoted the Bible. Not that there was anything wrong with being spiritual. Nate had just always thought of his dad as *street*, living by the code of the concrete jungle. Maybe that's why he himself had chosen the unruly bully path . . . because it's how he'd always pictured his father. Every son, at least at a young age, wanted to be their father when they grew up.

"I'm going to have to remember that," says Nathan, very serious.

"Don't just remember it, meditate on it day and night. Just so you'll have no excuses, we'll pick up a Bible for you."

Again, Nate had often dreamed about owning many a thing, but a Bible was not on the list. However, he had witnessed firsthand the joy and relief reading the Bible brought Ola Mae and Eva, and he assumed the Bible was the place where his father has found whatever it was he needed to be a man and a dad.

"Why can't I just use Me'ma's? That's what Granny Eva gave you all wrapped up," Nate slips, immediately slapping his hand over his mouth.

Nathaniel sighs.

"I'm sorry for spoiling the surprise."

"There's no need to be sorry, Nathan. I knew already. I just didn't have the heart to open it as of yet," he confesses.

"We can open it together when we get back home and you can show me the things you just told me," suggests Nate.

Nathaniel nods. "Do I really look like your Me'ma when I'm mad?" his father smiles.

"Like Me'ma with a fade," laughs Nathan.

"Let's grab a cab and get our tourist on! What do you want to see first?" exclaims Nathaniel, completely over being heated.

"The Apollo Theater."

Outside of the Apollo Theater, Nathan was paralyzed with pure amazement. The building itself was not fancy or polished but it radiated with inner beauty. The structure appeared strong in heritage. Nate tried to image the stars that got their big break on the stage inside. He also thought of the people who were booed but not broken by the animated Apollo crowd. Instead of letting getting dissed doom their dream, they stood and dared to strive.

Although the theater was a bit tarnished around the edges and on its sidewalk resided a little rubbish, it cried out pride. Black Pride. The Apollo could very well represent the young black man. Often judged by outward appearances, yet deep within is immeasurable potential and talent. If only someone would take the time to stop and venture inside, actually take notice of what it had to offer.

"I wish we could go in, son, but we can't."

"It's okay. I'm good with just standing outside. Who knows? Maybe one day I will be on Showtime at the Apollo. After all, the Good Book says *with God all things are possible*, right?" declares Nathan, hopeful.

"That's right, and you can do all things through Christ because He'll give you the strength," confirms Nathaniel, checking his watch. "We are going to have to be making tracks. It's getting late, we have to pick up something to eat and go back by the barbershop."

"I'm cool with that. I want to wait to see the Statue of Liberty and Empire State Building with Max and Granny Eva when they come. Can we take the subway? I want to see if it is like the ones in the movies?"

"Not this time, and Nathan I don't *ever* want you traveling the subway alone. It's not the safest place for a country boy."

CHAPTER THREE

Alone in a crowd!

Nathaniel wakes Nate early the next morning. "Get up Nathan. We have to get you enrolled in school."

"Okay."

Nathan hadn't had much time the night before to think about what it would be like to go to school in New York. But the more he thought about it now, the larger the butterflies in his stomach grew. He knew his social skills sucked. However, someone in the crowded city would befriend him . . . he hoped.

During the cab ride to school, Nathaniel tried to renew Nate's confidence in his personality by reminding him that everyone except Jesus had made mistakes. No matter what his father said, Nate still had his doubts about his likability. Yet he promised himself he would not go back to being Nate the Great. Before he did that, he'd become a loner, just a faceless nameless nobody.

"Dad, why do I have to go to this private school? Why can't I just go to the school two blocks from our house?" asks Nate, still uneasy.

"Nathan, we have been through this several times already this morning. Even though The Heights has improved plenty in terms of state of living, it still has a long way to go school wise. The sole purpose of going to school is to get the best possible education afforded to you. Going to school in The Heights poses too many distractions, the violence, the drugs . . . the lack of control.

There is so much chaos there you'd never be able to concentrate, and we both know concentration is vital to learning. Hill Street Academy is a private school but is not uptight. It provides organization and order. The environment you need to concentrate and learn. Remember, Nathan, I would never ever do anything to hurt you in any kind of way. Every decision I make is in your best interest. In time, you'll notice some familiar faces. Several other kids from our housing project go there."

Nathan said nothing else. What was there to say? He had no other choice but to do as his father said because he didn't want to end up being sent away.

Hill Street Academy was nothing like Doversville Middle School. Being a brick building was the extent of their similarities. For starters it was a two-story establishment. In fact, you could very well fit two of Doversville Middle Schools in the first floor of Hill Street Academy. And although the name sounded all prestigious and extravagant, the school was not. It was not half as polished as Nate's old school.

The hallway walls displayed pencil graffiti and several lockers have been beaten completely in. The floors are carpeted instead of tiled and inside the classrooms and cafeteria the chairs and tables had been bolted down.

"As you can see, Mr. Campbell, Hill Street Academy is not much to look at. But our academic achievement is remarkable. Slowly we are renovating our building to match our students and faculty," says the assistant principal, acting as a tour guide.

"Well, Ms. Carol, as my mama used to say, 'It's what's on the inside that counts' and Hill Street seems to have an academic heart of gold," replies Nathaniel.

"We definitely try. If you two will follow me this way, I will introduce you to Nathan's guidance counselor."

Nathan trekked along behind them surveying the place in detail, though his father and Ms. Carol are talking, he wasn't taking in much of their conversation nor was he the slightest bit interested.

"Knock, knock," declares Ms. Carol, tapping on one of the guidance counselor's doors. "Mr. Baiton, I have a new student here with me in need of your guidance," she announces lamely.

"Come in and I'll do my best to steer you in the right direction," says Mr. Baiton, a very tall thin man with a deep, deep voice. His voice and his body did not match; no one would ever expect such a powerful tone to bellow out of such a scrawny frame.

"This is Nathan," says Mr. Carol, introducing Nate first. " And this is his proud father, Nathaniel."

"Nice to meet you both."

"Same here," adds Nathaniel, but Nate maintains his silence.

"Nathan, if you'll have a seat, we'll see about getting you a class schedule," says Mr. Baiton, pointing to the chair in front of his desk.

"Here's his transcript, Mr. Baiton," declares Ms. Carol, placing a manila envelope before him.

"Thank you."

"Mr. Campbell, if you would accompany me to my office, we will complete all the remaining paperwork."

Nathan could hear Ms. Carol still chatting away as she and Nathaniel walk off.

"Okay Nathan. Let's see if we can't come up with the perfect class schedule for you using your transcript as our guide," says Mr. Baiton, browsing the contents of the folder.

"I can tell you right now I'm not real smart," confesses Nate.

"How would you know? From the looks of your records, you were rarely in your classes due to disciplinary problems. You have to be in class in order to complete assignments and make good or bad grades."

Until that moment, Nathan had never looked at his grade situation from that standpoint.

"You might be on to something, Mr. Baiton. My grades here will be much better because I don't plan on getting into any trouble. I wouldn't ever do anything to mess up my new start on purpose."

"That's good news, Nathan. Trouble is not welcomed here at Hill Street Academy, and I believe you were on the right track to turning over a new leaf right before you moved here. Your home-school grades reflect a vast improvement in your academic progress."

Instantly, Nathan thinks of Suzann. "I had a great teacher."

Nate and the guidance counselor spent the next half hour scheduling his classes and talking in general. Mr. Baiton advised Nathan not to be afraid to come to him for any reason, school related or personal. When they were done, he called Ms. Carol's office to see if she wants Nate sent straight to class. She doesn't. He was sent back to her office.

"I see you have a completed schedule," she says as he enters her office. "Are you comfortable with your class selections?"

"Yes ma'am."

"Mind if I take a look at it?" asks Nathaniel curiously.

"Go ahead," Nate replies, handing his father the printout.

"Woodshop?" Nathaniel says, surprised. "Hill Street offers woodshop?

"Yes sir we do, along with several computer courses like Powerpoint. We also have Advanced Home Economics, Agriculture, Expressions, which is voice and/or music classes and recently we add ballet. We want our students to have many intriguing and time-consuming electives. It builds perseverance and gives them something non-academic to look forward to everyday."

"I'm impressed! I wish they offered a few of those alternative electives in little Doversville, Georgia, where I went to school. You made a good choice though, son. I enjoyed woodshop, making things with my own two hands."

"I hope it's easy. I don't want to end up thumb-less or something," says Nate nervously.

"You'll be fine," assures his father. "I have to get going. Here's cab money and remember, you are to come to straight to the barbershop. Do *not* go to the apartment."

"Okay," Nate replies dryly.

"You're going to be fine, Nathan. You can do all things through Christ which strengthens you," Nathaniel declares, causing Nate to grin.

"Don't you worry either, Mr. Campbell. We ensure our cab riders' safety. We use one particular cab company, and an adult gives the cabby destination instructions. And for accountability purposes, we record the name of the driver, cab and tag number, and the name of the child or children who gets into each car daily."

"That's comforting to know. I was a little concerned about Nathan and the whole cab situation but he has to learn . . . he has to adapt to his new surroundings."

"See you at the shop, dad."

"Bye, son."

Ms. Carol escorted Nathan to his first class and introduced him. No one seemed to be moved one way or the other by his presence, and Nathan thanked God the teacher didn't embarrass him by making him stand and tell his classmates his name and where he's from. Since he hadn't made a ripple in the calmness of this course, he prayed he'd easily blend in to the point of being almost undetectable—like a chameleon.

And blend in was just what he did for his next two classes, absolutely no one paid much, if any, attention to the new kid. There are only twelve to fifteen students per class, but every seat was filled. Nothing about the kids that surrounded Nathan stood out to him. They were what Nate the Great would call *Average Cabbage*. If the school required the students to wear uniforms, the kids could easily be mistaken for robotic academic drones.

The lunch bell was music to Nate's ears. Whereas his academic appetite was entirely vanished, he was famished for food and the desire to get out of the classroom. Hill Street Academy's cafeteria was surprisingly small considering the school's size. It could only house two classes at a time. However, the variety of chow they provide was marvelous. They had a soup and salad bar, gourmet sandwich bar, a juice bar, an ice cream bar, a dessert buffet and a daily meal entrée.

In fact, they had so much to choose from, Nathan spent too much time deciding and by the time his lunch tray was to his satisfaction there are no more seats available. Nate circled the dining area several times, in hopes someone would either finish their food and vacate a chair or move their belongings and invite him to sit down. Indeed there were a few students who were done eating, but they were holding quiet conversations with their tablemates. Nathan decided to walk the lunchroom one last time before giving up.

As he approached the back of the cafeteria and the last round table, one of the students removes a backpack from a chair and nods toward the empty seat.

"Thanks," said Nate, truly relieved.

The student says nothing and just continued eating as if Nathan was not there.

Discreetly, Nate tried to size up this peculiar person. Whoever it was seemed to want to be more unnoticeable than he did. This person had on a boring gray sweatshirt-jacket with the hood on. Under the jacket's hood they wore a black skully, a matching black t-shirt along with a pair of light blue loose-fit jeans and sneakers. Most of the mystery person's face was hidden.

"My name is Nathan but most people call me Nate." Nathan says, in an honest attempt at making friends.

"I'm Chaz," the student blandly replies, getting up and leaving the table.

Nate was stunned. *"That went good,"* he tells himself sarcastically.

Nathan took his sweet time eating his lunch. What was the point of going outside to the atrium? No one would even talk to him. Shoot, the students weren't really talking to each other at all. From the looks of things, Hill Street Academy was a house of hermits. The only thing that could possibly redeem this school would be its' shop class, Nathan's last hope for fitting in. If the other kids never accepted him, at least woodshop would connect him to his father.

"Evening, class," declares the woodshop teacher. "We are going to pick up today right where we left off yesterday."

Nathan can't believe his ears. *"Duh, I wasn't here yesterday. What am I suppose to do?"*

"Why are you all still sitting around like knots on a log?" Mr. Fields snickers at his lumber plunder.

The children, without even a mere inkling of amusement, began to disburse, gathering safety gear and reporting to their respected stations.

Nathan stared aimlessly at Mr. Fields.

The shop teacher was Caucasian, average height but plump. He wore weathered steel-toe boots, khaki pants, and a too-little harvest green short sleeve button up shirt with a huge stain on the pocket. He was completely bald on the top of his head, but he combed his thinning hair from the side over the bald spot in an effort to conceal it. *Why do men do that?* Nathan thought to himself. *If you are bald on the top of your head, accept that you are bald on the top of your head. Trying unsuccessfully to hide it only draws more attention to it.*

Nathan slowly raised his hand. He no more wanted to bring attention to himself than Mr. Fields did his male pattern baldness.

But what choice did he have. The shop teacher hadn't taken roll or notice of a new face.

"I'm sorry youngster, I completely missed you back there. Are you new?"

"Nah, I just had plastic surgery. What a stupid question," Nate thought.

"Yes sir. Today is my first day."

"Okay," says Mr. Fields, walking over to where Nathan is seated. "Have you any experience with woodwork?"

"No sir," replies Nate, feeling like he is being examined underneath a high-powered microscope.

"Hmm, let me think for a minute," Mr. Fields declares, scratching the side of his swollen belly. "How about we pair you off with somebody for about a week, until you get a feel for things?"

Nate was not happy with the suggestion. The last thing in the world he wanted was to be paired with the breathing dead.

"I don't want to mess anybody up," says Nate.

"You won't be messing them up. You'll be helping them earn extra credit."

"Great, he has to bribe someone into showing me the ropes."

"Chaz!" yells Mr. Fields, walking towards the back room from which the humming of saws and drills was echoing.

Nathan remained immobile.

Not Chaz. Chaz had flat out rejected Nathan and there was no way he wanted to be partners with that kid.

Minutes later, Mr. Fields returns with Chaz by his side. "You're in luck, new kid. Chaz here has agreed to be your timber tutor," he announces, laughing uncontrollably.

Nathan and Chaz don't crack a smile.

"Get it? Timber tutor?" declares the shop teacher, still chuckling. But neither of the students shows the slightest interest in his effort at comedy. "I swear, video games have stripped you youngsters of humor! Anyhow, new kid, Chaz is the best in the school, second only to me. You're in good hands."

"Okay," Nate says reluctantly. "By the way, just in case you wanted to write it down in your roll book, my name is Nathan Campbell."

"Good thinking, new kid. I better go write that down now while it's still fresh on my mind. Wood is the only thing that gets my brain-saw buzzing." Mr. Fields chortles himself into tears.

"Grab some safety goggles and come on Nathan," says Chaz dryly.

So much for friendly banter. It was crystal clear to Nate this shop class was going to be a long one. Thank God it was the last of his school day.

"I miss Southern hospitality."

At their shared workstation, Chaz gives Nate one simple set of instructions. "Look, but don't touch!" and that's just what he does.

Nathan watched Chaz sculpt a wood work of art using only a grouter. The depths and dimension of the once two-by-four was quickly coming to life. Nathan wanted to ask several questions but was afraid to. After all, he had been advised to remain silent, plus he didn't want to break Chaz's concentration. When the bell rang to dismiss school, Nathan was relieved.

"I survived," he tells himself, walking out of the shop classroom and almost into Ms. Carol, the assistant principal.

"How was your first day here at Hill Street Academy?" she asks.

"Fine," he quickly answers, not interested in pow-wowing with authority figures.

"That's wonderful to hear. I've come to walk you through the cab riders' routine. It's very simple and I'm sure you won't have any problems catching on."

"Great!" Nathan says in his mind," *My dream has come true. My own personal chaperon."*

The whole cab rider procedure was self-explanatory. The children whose parents had completed the proper paperwork for their child to take a cab home did just that . . . take a cab home. Each cab rider student got into a cab, a few shared, the teacher on duty took down the cab driver's name, the cab's tag number, and the time of departure. Simple.

Nathan's destination was his father's barbershop. He hoped with all his heart was packed, that way his father would not have the opportunity to really grill him about his first day at school.

"I wonder what Max is doing right now. I bet he's tussling with Sam and Lucky," Nate smiles to himself. *"I wish I was there."*

"You were going to Clipper Creations Barbershop, right?"

inquires the cab driver, breaking up Nathan's daydreams of puppy play.

"Yes sir. How much do I owe you?"

"Nothing. They pre-pay your fare before you ever get into the cab. It's another way they try to keep tabs on your whereabouts."

"Thanks for the ride."

"No problem. That's my job. Tell your father I said hi."

"You know my dad?"

"I dropped you guys off the other night. I picked you from the airport, remember?"

Nathan takes a good look at the driver. "Sorry, I'm not very good with faces and with this city being so big all the faces are running together. It's all a blur. I don't really fit in here," he sighs.

"Don't worry, kid, it'll get better. Don't give up on the Big Apple just yet."

"I'll try, but it's hard when the Big Apple seems to be treating you like the worm."

"See you tomorrow."

Taking a deep breath, Nate entered his father's establishment.

"How was school, young Nathan?" asks Isaac.

Nathan quickly surveyed of the room for his father before he replied. He wanted to be extra careful to not even slightly sass the elder barber. Nathaniel was busy servicing a customer.

"Okay, Mr. Isaac."

"Okay! . . . just okay?" interjects B. "What up with that? I know better. Come on over here and tell me what the business really is. One player to another," Bryan chuckles, beating the bottom of his empty barber chair, freeing it of any clipper shavings and debris.

Nathan parks his rear in Bryan's chair and takes a long look at himself in the mirror. "My day was really just okay," he repeats.

"Com' on now, you expect me to believe that you only had an *okay* day. I know something happened worth talking about. You had to meet some interesting characters over there in savvy fancy Hill Street Academy."

"No, everybody kinda keeps to themselves there and it ain't all that fancy," sighs Nate.

"Dang young-blood, sorry to hear that," says Bryan, patting

Nathan on the shoulder. "Tell you what, how about I lower your ears for you. Preppy girls like clean cut dudes."

"It couldn't hurt."

Bryan shakes out his client cape a few times then wraps it around Nathan. "Hey Boss Man, you don't mind if I cut Junior's hair do you?"

"It's cool with me if it's cool with Nathan," replies Nathaniel.

Bryan begins brushing Nathan's hair, preparing it for cutting.

"B, I know a guy like you was popular in school. Maybe you can give me some pointers," whispers Nate.

"I wish I could, little dude, but fact is I quit school when I was about 14. I got a G.E.D four years later. But shoot, before I quit, I skipped class so much that when I did show up the teachers thought I was a new student," Bryan replies, smiling.

"That's funny, B. I *am* a new student and the teachers barely noticed me at all."

"Don't be discouraged, little man. You'll find your thang . . . your niche. We all do. With it comes the attention we want."

"Hope you're right."

"Com' on Nate, it's me, B. I would never shoot you a lie. Just stay in school and you'll see your boy Bryan knows what he is talking about."

The buzz of the clippers hum Nate into deep thought. He looked around the barbershop in the mirror. There were many men and boys here. Outside on the street were many passer-bys. In school, there were so many students. In the Heights Apartment buildings, there were so many tenants. *"How could anybody feel so alone in a place, a city, so crowded?"*

CHAPTER FOUR

The Great Fake

Embellishment quickly became the name of Nate's game. School once again had become a source of agitation for him. The only thing he did like about it was shop. Silent Chaz had taught him several key techniques for woodwork. After his week as a watcher, Nate began to work on his own and instantly found his niche. In shop, his workmanship spoke for him. He was still no Chaz, but Mr. Fields bragged that Nathan had great potential.

Bryan had been right. Find your niche and it would provide the attention desired. If it wasn't for the fact Hill Street Academy would soon be hosting a Wood Wonderland Workshop, Nate would have started skipping school. But perfect attendance was a requirement for participation in the show.

School was the only dead zone in Nathan's life. He and his father were getting along beautifully. Nathaniel had given Nate a job at the barbershop with a reasonable salary. Every day after school and for a few hours on Saturday Nathan was in charge of shop sanitation. He swept and mopped the floors, wiped down the mirrors and countertops, and cleaned the bathroom. In just a few short weeks, he had saved a good bit of money to spend when Eva and Max arrived to go sightseeing.

In spite of the fact he had yet to make friends in school, Nathan had picked up a few new pals from the neighborhood. His new friends were nothing like his buddy, Max from back home. Max Andrews was the cookie cutter 'boy-next-door' and Nathan's new friends, well they were trendsetters. They took pride in not fitting in and standing out. Nate's new crew thrived off being different and 'different' was a language Nathan spoke well. In the dialect of different, Nathan was deemed Knick Nate, kind of like Knick Knack because the fellas knew how much he loved making things out of wood. Plus, being tall and lanky, a couple of the guys thought Nate could easily one day play for the New York Knicks.

Over the course of several weeks, Nate gradually talked his father into dating the lovely Sydney. Although Nathaniel vowed to take things really slow with Syd, Nathan knew his father was smitten with her and she with him. Neither could hide it. Nathan really liked Sydney as well. She was cool. She played videos games and taught him to shoot pool, but more importantly she never tried to be his mother. Why shouldn't his father have someone to spend his time with? With Sydney in the picture Nathan, would have a lot more free time on his hands. Time he planned to spend chilling with his new buds.

"That's a mighty fine piece of art there, Nathan," says Mr. Fields, interrupting Nate's thoughts.

"Thanks."

"You're a real quick study. You caught right on. That Chaz is an excellent teacher."

Nathan just nods in agreement, wishing Mr. Fields would mosey on to the next workstation.

"Chaz," yells the shop teacher before strolling away, "Ol' Nathan over here is going to give you a run for you money in the Wonderland Workshop this year."

After school, Nate falls into place with the other cab riders. "What's up, Knick Nate," someone calls out from across the street.

"Hey Raw. What are ya'll doing here?"

"Leaving the premises," responds Ms. Carol, giving Nathan's friends a stern glare.

"We'll catch you back at the spot," growls Raw, snarling at Ms. Carol.

"Does your father know you are associating with the likes of those delinquents?" the assistant principal asks.

What does she mean delinquents? She doesn't even know, Raw and War. Just because they dress a certain way and talk differently doesn't make them delinquents. They hadn't judged the students at Hill Street, so why was Mr. Carol so quick to judge them?

Raw and War are mirror twins and that's how they got their nicknames. What is raw in a mirror . . . war. The twins were descent boys, or at least Nate thought so. They, along with the rest of the

Heights Knights had befriended him when not a soul in the Hill Street stuck-up-silence *asylum* would.

"Aright fellas, I have to run by the barbershop first," Nate hollers, completely ignoring Mr. Carol's question.

"The next cab is yours Nathan," instruct Ms. Carol, pointing. "I suggest you think carefully about your choice of friends."

"I suggest you mind your own business," Nate murmurs under his breath, slamming the cab door.

"How's it going today, young Nathan?" asks husky Sal, who has become Nate's regular ride.

"It would be a whole lot better if people would mind their own business," he snaps, still fuming from Ms. Carol's judgment of his friends.

The cab driver takes silent for a moment. "I didn't mean to pry," sighs Sal, "I was only trying to make conversation."

Nathan realizes his statement is misunderstood, "Oh no, Mr. Sal, I was not talking about you. I was talking about Assistant Principal Carol. She said my friends are delinquents and she doesn't even know them."

"Oh," the driver replies, almost relieved. "Well Nathan, even though it doesn't always seem like it, grownups try to look out for your best interest. Maybe she knows something about your friends that you don't."

"Nah, maybe I made a mistake by thinking you would understand. You are an adult and ya'll always stick together," Nate snarls in his thoughts."

"I doubt it," he says aloud.

Nathan remains quiet until the cab safely arrives at the barbershop. As he gets out, he tells Sal he'll see him later.

Inside Clipper Creations, business is booming. There are customers all over the place. "Hey Nathan, how was school," asks Mr. Isaac as usual.

"What's with people always sweating me?" Nate thinks to himself.

"Nathan, tell Mr. Isaac about the Wood Wonderland Workshop coming up," interjects Nathaniel excitedly.

"Thanks a lot, dad. I don't want to talk about the workshop . . . I don't want to talk period!"

"Hill Street is having a wood workshop and the students get to show off what we've been doing in woodshop. I'm going to enter a few of my pieces, why don't you come, Mr. Isaac? Then you'll see I'm good with more than a broom and dust pan," states Nate dryly.

"I'd be honored, Nathan. You can count me in."

"Hey, lil' brother, what about me? I know you ain't going to leave your big brother B out. Where's my invite?" inquires Bryan.

"You know you can come too, B. We cool like that. In fact everybody in the barbershop is invited to my school's Wonderland Workshop," Nate declares loudly.

All the folks in earshot erupt in laughter.

"That boy of yours is something else," chuckles the customer in Nathaniel's chair.

"That he is. Now be still and stop laughing before I gap up your head."

"When you gone get another barber in here to fill that empty station? What are you doing, waiting on that boy of yours to grow up and follow in your footsteps?" asks the customer, ignoring Nathaniel's request to be still.

Nathaniel smiles politely. He didn't want his son to follow in his footsteps or remotely in his twisted trodden path. He wanted so much more for Nathan.

"Nah, Nathan really hasn't shown any interest in the family business. Whatever he chooses, his old man is going to stand firmly behind him. Anyhow, that chair won't be vacant too much longer."

Nate rushes to complete his duties as the shop's sanitation supervisor. Funny, his father has given him the title supervisor when he is the *only* one *officially* working sanitation. When Nathan asked his father about his job title, Nathaniel simply replied, "Son, you supervise the broom and mop across the floor and the application of Windex to the mirrors and countertops."

Jokingly, Nathan responded by asking his father if he could hire some help and wisely his father informed Nate he already had a staff of four . . . his hands and feet.

"Where's the fire, Sidekick?" asks Nathaniel, referring to Nathan's hasty cleanup.

"There's no fire, dad," Nate proclaims, trying to downplay his anxiousness. "I just wanted to get home a little early to make sure the apartment is really clean for Sydney's birthday dinner tonight. That's all."

Nathaniel stops and stares at his son.

"What's wrong, dad?"

"Nothing. I'm just so proud of you and how thoughtful and responsible you are becoming. Way to man-up."

"I have a great teacher," Nate says, winking and returning to duties.

The minute his last chore was done, Nathan hurriedly bid everyone an early goodbye and hailed a cab home. He hoped he wouldn't miss his friends, but he does by mere minutes.

"Good evening, Nathan," says Mr. Dan, manning the complex's security gate.

"Hey," Nate replies grouchily.

"Now is that any way to greet a friend?" inquires Mr. Dan, noticing Nathan's glum attitude.

Nate doesn't bother to respond.

"If your little 'tude is about your little buddies, they came by here, even tried to hang around waiting on you but I made them leave. They got no business posting up around here. Those hoodlums are nothing but trouble and you need not socialize with the likes of them."

"You ran my friends off," Nate steams angrily, backtracking in the direction of the security gate.

"Yeah I made them scat and I'll do it again. In fact, I'm going to run them off every time they trot their little raggedy behinds over here."

"Who do you think you are?" Nate challenges Mr. Dan.

"I'm your friend. Real friends look out for the best interests of one another."

"No! You're an old man trying to run my life! You are not my friend and you are not my grandpa either! Remember that!" yells Nate, headed towards the apartment building again.

"Oh, I'll remember that alright . . . I'll remember it when you want some of my Cora's homemade cookies, you little ingrate! You just remember we are not friends when your little cronies get you in hot water!"

Nathan slams the apartment door so hard a framed snapshot of him, his father and Sydney falls off the wall.

"Damn!" he exclaims, flopping down on the sofa unconcerned with the picture. "Why can't folks just leave me alone? I know dumb ol' Mr. Dan is going to tell dad about Raw 'em!"

"You can't go out like this," instigates Nathan's dark side. *"You gotta pull the great fake. You can't afford to lose your New York friends. Sure good ol' Max is coming to visit, but you gotta remember he's just visiting. Then he's going home to Georgia."*

Nate the Great had returned, picking up right where he had left off. Nathan Campbell was weak and submissive but Nate the Great was a fearless warrior, a go-getter. Unlike Nathan, Nate the Great did not wait for things to happen . . . Nate the Great *made* them happen.

Nathan nods to himself, "True. True."

Nate the Great continues, *"Even if nosey Mr. Dan does tell on you, you can use Max and Granny Eva to undermine him . . . you know, show your father your only friends are Max and Eva, him and Syd."*

Instantly, Nathan's conscience has a revelation, *"Nate, if your new friends are not delinquents, then why the secrecy."*

"It's not secrecy, it's privacy," he thinks aloud, shaking off the seeding feeling of guilt. "Now, to get this place in tip top shape," he says, uprooting himself from the couch and bending over the picture.

After returning the picture to its place, Nathan took a quick shower, vacuumed and dusted. Feeling renewed by his conversation with himself, Nathan's mood had drastically improved. He was no longer gloomy. He was on top of the world. In fact, he was in such a good mood, he prepared the refreshments, lit a few scented candles and puts out all the party favors before his father got home to cook Sydney's birthday buffet.

"Looks and smells good, Sidekick!" declares Nathaniel, surveying the place. "Appreciate you decorating the place. Now I can concentrate on baking your grandma Ola Mae's secret recipe—melt-in-your-mouth pound cake."

"Sounds delish," says Nate, licking his lips remembering just how good his Me'ma's cakes were.

"I'ma hit the shower first, son. Could you do me a favor and run over to Mr. Dan's and see if Cora is finished with the pot roast and potatoes. Miss Syd's taste buds aren't going to know what hit them! Deep South soul food will have the girl licking her fingers," Nathaniel proclaims overjoyed.

Nathan stood paralyzed. How could he possibly face Mr. Dan after the ugly confrontation they'd had earlier? *Nathan* couldn't face Mr. Dan, but slick Nate the Great could.

"Get going, Nathan. I'm going to need your help with the rest of the menu."

"Okay, Dad. I have to put on my shoes."

Outside of the Dan's apartment, Nathan Campbell disappeared and Nate the Great knocked on the door.

"Who is it?" roars Mr. Dan, like an irritated grizzly bear.

"Nathan," replies Nate the Great, confident he can handle his neighbor.

"What do you want," snaps Mr. Dan, opening the door wide? Your little buddies already got you in hot water?"

"No silly, get out the way," says Cora, pushing her husband to the side. "He's here to see me. Come on in, Nathan."

"Oh I get it," chuckles Mr. Dan, sarcastically. "You don't want to be my friend because you're after my woman."

"Ignore him. He's just grouchy because the doctor put him on a low calorie diet and he hasn't had anything sweet in almost a week," giggles Cora, leading Nathan to the kitchen.

"Don't kid yourself, Snuckcums. You got all the sugar I need."

Cora rolls her eyes, "Here you go baby, so you can get on out of here. I know you don't want to hear an old crusty man whispering sweet nothings. Be careful cause it's hot. You can just bring the pot holders back tomorrow."

"Bring what potholders back tomorrow?" asks Mr. Dan, getting up from his recliner to investigate the transaction taking place in the kitchen.

"These potholders," says Nate the Great slyly.

"Whoa now, Cora, the boy can have the potholders for all I care, but he needs to leave that pot roast. I thought that was our dinner."

"How many times have I got to tell you, honey, don't think. You'll just give yourself a headache to go along with your long list of other ailments. The pot roast is for Nathaniel. He's making a birthday dinner for Sydney and I offered to help him out."

"But . . . but–" Mr. Dan stammers.

"But nothing. Nathan you get home and help your father. Joseph Dan, you go park it in your rickety recliner and I'm going to serve you a Zestations salad on a TV tray."

"Thank you. I'll be sure to bring your potholders back tomorrow, Mrs. Dan. Enjoy your salad, Mr. Dan," gloats Nate the Great.

"It's about time you got back. Just sit that on top of the stove so that it will stay warm. Then butter the sheet cake pan really good 'cause I'm almost finished mixing this batter. After you finish buttering the pan, I need you to prepare the salad and last, run to the store and grab a bag of ice."

"Sir, yes sir!" laughs Nate.

Together Nate and Nathaniel pull together a spectacular intimate birthday bash for Sydney. "Nathan, grab ten bucks off my nightstand and hurry back with the ice. Syd will be here any minute now."

"I'll be back in a flash."

Nate scurried from the apartment complex, hoping he would run across his pals. But to his disappointment, they were nowhere in sight. Inside the Minute Mart, Nate literally runs into Chaz.

"Watch where you are going, woodworm!"

Chaz looks right through Nathan as if he isn't even standing there and walks off. Which only angers him further.

"Yeah you better keep stepping, looking like a sissy girl."

Those inflammatory words didn't seem to faze Chaz. Truth be told, nothing ever seemed to faze Chaz and that really annoyed Nathan. He wanted Chaz to acknowledge his presence. After all, he was Knick Nate . . . shoot, he was Nate the Great. Busters bowed down to him and Chaz was going to realize real soon there were no exceptions to that rule.

The clock above the clerk's head catches Nathan's eye. "You don't mind if I cut in front of you," he says, shoving Chaz out of the way and putting the bag of ice on the counter.

The clerk looks at Chaz for any sign of resistance to Nate's rudeness, but there is none. So she rings up the ice for Nate. She doesn't want him in her store a moment longer than necessary anyway.

Nate the Great sprints from the Minute Mart towards home.

"Knick Nate!" a voice calls out from the shadows just as Nathan reaches The Heights security gate, stopping him cold in his tracks.

"Yeah," Nate replies in a macho voice, just in case somebody wants trouble.

Raw and War burst into laughter, "You can take the bass out of your voice. It's only us, Mr. Tough-guy."

"What's up? I thought I might run across ya'll."

"You got a minute?" asks the twins simultaneously.

"I always got time for my homies," Nate the Great replies, crossing the street to where his buddies are posted up.

"We want you to meet someone," they announce, separating and revealing a new face.

"Raw and War have told me nothing but good things about you, Knick Nate," says an older guy who has the same kind of apple tattoo as Bryan.

"What's up?" says Nate.

"I came here to ask you the same thing. As I just said, the Terrible Two here have been bragging about you. I wanted to meet you and see what's really up with you. You know, see if you are really down . . . see for myself what you are all about."

Nate the Great just glares at this new character, already knowing where this conversation is headed.

"My name is Jyran, but everybody whose somebody calls me J-ran."

"J-ran is the man around here," declares Raw.

"Yeah he runs these streets," adds War.

"Cool," states Nate in admiration.

"So what's up Knick Nate? Are you in or out?" inquires J-ran.

Nathan looks puzzled.

J-ran pulls him close and speaks. Raw and War walk a few paces away from them. "It's like this, little man. I run the Heights Knights. Now see, you have been hanging with some of my young bloods over there, reaping the benefits of gang living without being a member. I can't let that continue . . . it makes me look bad. So you see, I need to know do you want to really be a Heights Knight, 'cause if you don't, you gone have to step off and leave my boys over there alone. You feel me?"

Nathan doesn't even give the decision a half second thought, "What do I have to do to become a real member of the Heights Knights?"

J-ran smiles, "Your eager spirit is a great start."

Nathan smiles proudly, "Back in the day, they didn't call him Nate the Great for nothing."

"Nate the Great, huh? I like that. It has a nice ring to it. You in or out, *Nate the Great?*"

"I'm in."

"Good answer."

Chaz walks by and the gang grows quiet. "I can't stand that woodworm right there," barks Nathan.

"You just gave me an idea, Knick Nate. I think we can work out your little social problem during your initiation."

"Good, as they say where I'm from, let's kill two birds with one stone."

"Nathan!" shouts Sydney from the security gate.

Nate was frozen. How much had Sydney witnessed?

"I'm coming," he says, as she crosses the street to where he is, walking right up to J-ran.

Raw and War come to attention and stand one on each side of Sydney. She laughs, "Call off your guard puppies, Jyran, before I beat them until they are house broken."

"It's cool, guys. Syd is harmless."

"We both know that's not true. Don't let the dress and the makeup fool you, because underneath I am still a country girl and you know *we* don't play. Stay away from Nathan, Jyran. I'm not joking. Or else I'm going to remind you how harmful I can be when provoked."

"I'll get up with you later with the details on what we were talking bout," J-ran tells Nate.

"Come on, Nathan. Let's go!" demands Sydney.

"They were just asking me for directions," Nathan lies once they have cleared The Heights security gate.

Sydney's hasty footsteps halt. She looks Nate square in the eye. "Do you think I'm stupid enough to believe that? You've been here what . . . a few months. Jyran and the double mint twins were born and raised here. Why would they ask *you* for directions? Listen to me and listen good. Stay far, far away from Jyran and I mean it. If I even think you've been anywhere near him or his little crew, I will tell your father and we both know you don't want that."

She had a point and Nate the Great knew she meant business. Country girls never made idle threats.

"Deal," he embellished.

"Good," Sydney replies, running her fingers through her disheveled hair and straightening her figure framing dress. "Let's go see what your dad has hooked-up for my birthday."

And that's just what they do, as if the confrontation with J-ran had not taken place. *"Sydney really is cool,"* Nate the Great tells himself, as they feast on her savory birthday cake. Anybody else would have ratted him out without ever considering giving him a second chance.

"This cake is awesome," proclaims Sydney, helping herself to another slice.

"My mama's secret recipe," admits Nathaniel.

"Boy, your mama could have made Betty Crocker suicidal. Her secret recipe is killer."

Nathaniel and Nathan laugh at Sydney's seriousness.

"Gift time," announces Nathaniel, producing a beautifully wrapped box from the coat closet.

"I would have been satisfied with just this cake."

"Well, in that case, I can always take it back," jokes Nathaniel, pretending to put it back in the closet.

"If you don't give me that box, I'ma hurt you."

"Dad, you better give it to her. I think she can take you," chuckles Nathan.

"I think you might be right, Sidekick. Here you go, Syd. I hope you like it."

She takes the box and slowly begins to unwrap it. The anticipation is killing Nathaniel and Nathan.

"You need some help with that grandma?" asks Nathaniel in a creaky voice.

"Oh I could always wait until I get home to open it. Right, Nathan?"

"Yes you could, but please don't. I'm dying to see what it is," pleads Nate, getting down on his knees and clasping his hands together.

"For you and you alone Nathan I'm going to go ahead and open it here," says Sydney, winking.

Hidden in the present's interior is a baby blue smock with Syd embroidered on the right breast pocket.

Nathaniel begins to explain, "You've been complaining about working clear across town. You know the commute is awful. Anyway there's an empty chair at Clipper Creations with your name on it if you want it. We need someone who can cornrow, twist and do locks."

Before he can speak another word, Sydney plants a wet one on Nathaniel.

"I'd say that's a definite yes," snickers Nate, uneasily.

He had never seen his father kiss anyone and wasn't really sure how he felt about Sydney filling his mother's dream shoes, working side by side with his father.

"Is that a yes?" inquires Nathaniel, wanting to hear the actual word.

"Yes!" exclaims Sydney. "Yes! Yes! Yes! Thank you Bae."

"You're more than welcome, Syd. I think this calls for some Champagne!"

"None for me," Nathan says sarcastically, "I'm going to leave you kids to celebrate."

CHAPTER FIVE

Old friend, new foe

Finally the day had come. Max and Eva were scheduled to arrive any second. Nathaniel and Sydney were already in route to meet Gilbert, Eva's brother and his wife Mary Jean, to pick them up. Nathan had volunteered to stay behind and hang decorations, including a 'Welcome to New York' banner. Actually, he wanted to be alone for a while. It had been several months since he had even spoken to Max and he wasn't quite sure how he felt about seeing him again. Truth be told, he'd even forgotten the prayer Eva had made up for them.

Max was every parent's dream child, well-behaved and made very good grades. Nate always felt inferior when he compared himself to Max. His friend from back home was everything he was not. It was cold living in Max's shadow. Nate the Great despised goody-two shoes Maxwell Andrews Jr. and lately Nate the Great had been running Nathan's show.

The sound of keys jingling draws Nathan from his insecure thoughts. "Son, look what the cat drug in!"

"Come on over here and act like you still love me," exclaimed Eva, looking every bit the grandma diva she was. "Give me a hug, you handsome devil you."

"It's so good to see you, Granny Eva," Nathan sighs honestly. Eva's embrace reminds him of Ola Mae's. He had almost forgotten how much he missed his Me'ma.

"Hey, I missed you too," laughs Max, pulling Nathan and Eva apart and revealing a small gift.

"You didn't have to get me anything," Nate says modestly and a little uncomfortable. Max has always been considerate and kind, nothing like his new self-serving friends. It is proving to be a real task to pretend to be nice.

"Where is your room? Let's try it out," says Max, revealing the gift was a video game.

"Follow me."

"Well, Miss Sydney, sit down and tell me how my boys have been behaving. From the looks of 'em, you have been taking mighty good care for them," says Eva, patting the sofa next to her.

"I'm going to get you ladies a glass of ice tea," Nathaniel offers.

"I see you haven't lost your Southern charm," giggles Eva the Grandma Diva.

"What can I say? You can take the boy out the country but you can't take the country out the boy."

Nathaniel serves the women folk and peeks in on Nathan and Max. He finds himself disturbed by what he sees. The boys aren't fussing or fighting, but they are not talking or laughing either. They are playing the video game in complete silence.

"What's wrong with this picture?" he asks himself. *"What happened?"* Nathaniel thinks back to the days before he and Nathan left Georgia. Nathan and Max had been thick as thieves, inseparable. No one could get a word in edgewise around the two of them.

"You guys doing okay?" he asks, tapping on the door revealing his presence.

"Yes sir," they sigh unenthused.

"Can I get you anything?"

"Nah, dad, we are good."

"Okay. If you change your minds, I'll be in my room. Eva and Sydney have the living room on lock with their girl talk."

"Thanks for the warning," says Max.

"Don't stay up too late. Tomorrow Eva plans to take you guys to Ellis Island."

"Yes sir," they resound, again uninterested.

Several hours later Eva checks in on the boys as she had done many times before back home in Georgia. "How's it going, fellas?"

"Fine," Max replies blandly.

"Well it sure as heck doesn't sound like it."

"Really, we are doing okay," says Nathan.

"Boy, you can't slick this ol' can of oil. Put that game away, come over here and let's talk."

They do as they are told and take their respective places by Eva's side. "You boys haven't even been separated six months. Don't tell me you're already growing apart?"

"Me and Max, we still cool, Granny Eva."

"Correction, Nathan, you and Max are not cool. Your friendship is downright cold."

"Things are so different here. Nothing like Doversville. We really don't have much to talk about," declares Nate, trying to convince Eva.

"If things are so different then you and Max should have plenty to talk about. You can tell him all about big city living and he can bring you up to speed on his neck of the woods."

"Wood!" Nathan thinks. *"Perfect subject change."*

"Well I guess I can start by telling you about this woodshop class I'm taking in school."

"Sounds like a perfect place to start," says Eva, getting up to leave them. "I have to go say goodnight to Nathaniel. He just kicked me and Sydney off the couch, saying he had to get to bed. I sure hate putting him out of his own room, but an old woman like me can't sleep on nobody's sofa. My back would be in knots by morning."

"She hasn't changed a bit."

"Why would she?" asks Max. "She *is* Eva the Grandma Diva."

Nathan mentions everything he can possibly think of concerning woodwork. Excitement overtakes him as he describes the pieces he plans to display at the Wood Wonderland Workshop. He even promises to surprise Eva by sending her the spice rack he made.

"I wish we could stay long enough to attend the wood workshop, but I have to get back for school. It sounds interesting. Maybe I'll try to get into a shop class next year as an elective."

Wow, Nathan was in awe. Max wanted to do something he was doing? What a refreshing change.

"I guess we should call it a night. Like Granny said, 'we have a long day ahead of us tomorrow.'"

"Night, Max."

"Night, Nathan."

Bright and early the next morning, Eva was up making good use of the Campbell's small kitchen. She hooked them up a large breakfast and man did they appreciate it. Living in bachelor bliss meant eating cereal and instant oatmeal and grits on the regular. Fluffy pancakes, scrambled eggs, crisp thick bacon, and chilled orange juice were a welcomed change.

"Eva, you are spoiling us. We are never going to want you to leave."

"I have that effect on men," laughs Eva, laying two hot pancakes fresh off the griddle on Nathaniel's plate.

"I bet you do. They say the way to a man's stomach is through his stomach."

"Amen, Amen. Don't worry, I have a feeling home-cooking is in your very near future. I bet that Sydney can rattle some pots."

"Nathan and I have yet to sample her cooking. She owes us one though because me and my Sidekick over there got down with her big birthday dinner. I made her a melt-in-your-mouth cake from Mama's secret pound cake recipe."

"I sure I hate I missed that. You should have saved me a piece of that cake so I could see if you did Ola Mae's recipe justice."

"I think she would have approved," Nathaniel smiles warmly, thinking of his mother.

"What do you think, Nathan? Was your father's cake that good?" asks Eva.

Nate pauses for a few minutes, acting as if he is trying to ponder over the issue. "Well . . . ."

"Sidekick? I thought you had your old man's back," chuckles Nathaniel.

"I was just teasing you, dad. Your cake was so good you could open a bakery. Me'ma would have been proud."

"Oh, now you're being sarcastic. I'm going to remember that come Christmas," kids Nathaniel, clearing his place at the table. "Max, you would have backed Maxwell wouldn't you?"

Max laughs, "My dad can cook but he *cannot* bake."

"Ohhh, I'm gonna tell him when we get back," taunts Eva.

"Granny, don't you know? What happens in New York stays in New York."

"The boy has a point," says Nathaniel, aiding Max.

"I see how ya'll are. You men are sticking together this morning."

"I got to get to the barbershop. Sydney's waiting for me outside in her car."

"If it's alright, we are going to stop by and check out your shop after we get our tourist-on."

"Please do. We'll roll out the red carpet for you," replies Nathaniel, trotting to the door. "Now one last time, Sydney's still offering you all her car to get around in today."

"How can we be tourists riding around in a car with New York plates. Today we are traveling by cab, subway and ferry."

Nathaniel throws his hands up in surrender, "I guess that means I'll see you at the barbershop later this evening."

"You boys enjoy the rest of your breakfast. I'm going to transform this grandma into a snowcapped diva."

Ellis Island was nothing like Nathan had imagined. Although Eva and Max seemed to really be enjoying the sites, Nate's heart really wasn't in it. He'd rather be somewhere, anywhere, with his new friends. He tried to fake gusto for pictures but didn't fool Max.

"You really don't want to be here do you?" he asks.

"It's not that. I just . . . I just . . . I don't know."

"You want to talk about it?"

Nathan doesn't really want to talk about it, but he knows he has to tell Max something to get him off his back.

"Not in front of Granny Eva."

"You don't have to worry about her. She'll be cooing over that lady's baby over there for the next thirty minutes," says Max, knowing his grandmother has never met a stranger.

"Okay, let's step over here to the side."

Max follows Nathan a few feet away from Eva, "Don't you guys wander too far," she warns.

"We won't," they yell together.

"So what's up, Nathan? You don't really like it here do you?" inquires Max.

Nate thinks for a moment before he answers. "Nah, I like it here just fine. The people don't seem to like me though."

Max listens attentively, remembering not too long ago he knew that feeling well.

"For instance, there's this flunky named Chaz. Always walking 'round here like I don't even exist. Won't even acknowledge my presence. I mean this jack-in-the-box won't even speak when spoken to."

"Did it ever occur to you this Chaz person might be really, really shy."

"Nope Max, Chaz ain't shy. Chaz is just a a–"

"Hey Knick Nate?" hollers War.

"What are you guys doing here?" asks Nathan, wary. He had never planned on his old friend and new ones ever meeting.

"Dang, you acting like you scared to talk to us around," Raw stops and looks Max up and down, "around whoever this square is."

Max takes a defensive stance.

"It's nothing like that man. Let me introduce ya'll," Nate the Great says, quickly trying to defuse the situation. "Raw, War, this is Max, my friend from back home and Max these two are my New York homies."

Max looks at Raw and War as if they are contagious.

"Ah, Knick Nate you better check this square's staring problem before we dice 'em diagonal and make 'em two triangles," warns Raw.

"See there, you did learn something in school," snickers War, "two triangles make a square."

Nathan chuckles, "Like I said, what are you cats doing here?"

"Chillin, looking for some quick cash to grab a bite to eat. We ain't got nothing better to do right now. The question is what are you doing here? You claimed you never wanted to visit the tourist traps."

Max glares at Nathan with growing anger. If Nate didn't want him and Eva to visit, he should have said so, and they could have remained in Jersey for the length of their trip, around people who desired their company.

"You better be real careful how you answer that," Max snarls to himself.

"I told you my old pal Max is visiting. We had already talked about checking out Ellis Island before he came."

"Whatever!" snaps War. "Sounds like you are riding the post pony. Either you like the sites or you don't, just like either you are a Heights Knight or you ain't."

Nate the Great is speechless. He wants to denounce Max and the stupid tourist sites but he knows if he disses them, Eva will report his behavior to Nathaniel.

"Let's go, War. We ain't got time for no babies. See that ol' bag right there running her trap," says Raw nodding towards Eva, "let's snatch her purse and go get a pizza."

Max pushes Nathan to the side and boldly stands up for his grandmother. "I wish you would try it!"

"What? Fool have you lost your freaking mind?" growls War.

"Hey, Knick Nate. You better tell your buddy who he's messing with, before we take his money, too, for dessert!" threatens Raw.

"Whoa, Raw . . . War, that's Max's granny. You wouldn't let nobody rob your granny without a fight."

"I wouldn't care if it was his great, great greasy queasy grandma. He better watch how he rolls up on us."

"Oh you would care after I finished with you, you'd take off running anytime you heard the word granny," spews Max, ready to explode.

"Punk country boy, who do you think you are? We ain't in the back woods of Georgia," boasts War.

"I am Maxwell Rashod Andrews Jr., but I'm about to bring Mad Max out of retirement. You're making me angry . . . and I'm not responsible for my actions when I'm angry!"

"Chill! Chill!" Nate intervenes, getting between Max and Raw. "Check this out, pizza and dessert is on me," he says, placing most of his hard earned barbershop money in Raw's hand.

"You lucky dork. Knick Nate just bought you a reprieve," snaps Raw, backing up.

"Nah, you're the one lucky. Nathan just bought you another day among the living. Talking about robbing my granny."

"Com' on War," demands Raw, pulling his twin, "We better make tracks now before I stomp this punk and then rob his precious granny just for the hell of it."

"We'll catch up with you later, Knick Nate . . . when you're not guarded by your mama," spits War, as he turns to stroll off with his brother.

Nate didn't appreciate the comment about his mama too much.

He was going to have to make it known amongst his new pals his mother was a topic they had better tap dance around.

"Some kind of friends, talking about your dead mother," declares Max, still upset.

"Careful there, pot-calling-the-kettle-black. You talked trash about my mama too, and for your information they don't know my mama's dead," Nate states, leaving Max to flashback.

Max had said some things about Nathan's mother before they had become friends, when they were feuding foes.

"Granny Eva," Nate says, drawing her attention from her conversation and the chubby cheeked baby.

"Yes, Mr. Nathan?"

"I'm not feeling too good. Seeing all these kids with their mother's is making me miss my Me'ma. Can we go?"

Compassion overtakes Eva and she wraps her arms around Nathan. "Of course we can. It was nice to meet ya'll and if you are ever in Georgia, look me up," she tells the mother pushing the cute baby girl in a pink stroller.

"Sorry Nathan," Max whispers.

"Don't be sorry," Nate the Great declares in his mind, *"just be gone!"*

Nathan no longer wanted to be around Max. He no longer wanted to be his acquaintance. As far as Nate was concerned, his old friend had become his new foe . . . again.

CHAPTER SIX

Invitation for Initiation

Nathan had not spoken to Max or Eva since their departure from New York. It had been very awkward during their last few days together. Eva had picked up on the rift between them, but in spite of all her grandma diva magic she was unable to fix it.

Lately, Nate's main concern was the Wood Wonderland Workshop. It was all he had left. He had not seen or heard a single peep out of Raw or War. He figured they had told J-ran what happened on Ellis Island and the gang had washed their hands of him. As soon as the Wonderland Workshop was over, Nate the Great planned to become Kermit the Hermit. No school, no socializing, no need to see the light of day.

"Nathan, I am looking forward to your presentation tomorrow," declares Mr. Isaac, sweeping hair clippings into the dustpan Nate was holding.

"I can't wait either. Part of me is excited and the other part of me is nervous and just wants to get it over with," he says, dumping the dustpan contents into the wastebasket.

"Well if it's any consolation, everybody has at one time or another been at least a little bit nervous when they are doing or showcasing something they love," Mr. Isaac confesses, sitting down in Bryan's barber chair.

"I've never done nothing like this before. The only time I've had to address the principal and students and their parents was when I was in trouble," confides Nate the Great, wishing Mr. Isaac will wave a magic wand of wisdom and unknowingly undo all of his troubles.

The old man laughs, silently thinking back to some times when he found himself in a nervous bind. "Nathan," he chuckles aloud, "I wish you could have seen me after finishing my very first haircut as a professional barber . . . on a paying customer. Back in those days we gave the client a hand mirror to overlook their new do.

I tell you, youngster, the whole time I was cutting my customer's hair I was fine. I was comfortable and wasn't nervous whatsoever. But the moment the minute arrived for me to show him my handy work, my hand began to shake and I almost dropped the mirror when I gave it to him."

"That's hard to believe, Mr. Isaac," interjects Bryan. "Watching you cut hair the way you do people would think you were born with a pair of humming clippers in your hand."

"I wish it were so. I love cutting hair. I love providing a service that makes others feel good about themselves. But to this day I'm always a little uneasy about presenting my clients the end product."

"Wow," thinks Nate, *"Me and Mr. Isaac have something in common."*

Nathan loved to do wood work. It was as natural to him as breathing and as soothing as his Me'ma, Ola Mae, singing her favorite hymn. But he was extremely anxious about presenting the fruit of his hands to the world, well his world, Hill Street Academy.

"Try this one on for size, Sidekick," says Nathaniel, getting in on the storytelling. "Imagine making a spice rack for your Me'ma. We both know how much you loved and respected your grandma. Think about how much you would want for it to be perfect and how much you would want to please her and not let her down."

Nate thinks about it intensely. Making a spice rack for Ola Mae would have been nerve racking.

"That feeling in the pit of your gut right now is exactly how I felt when my very first paying client happened to be my esteemed mentor . . . Mr. Isaac. Man was I uptight. I wanted every buzz of the clippers to be just right. I didn't want to let him down."

"Dad, you cut Mr. Isaac's hair?" Nate states in awe, not being able to fathom the pressure of such a task.

"He sure did, Nathan . . . that's why I let my hair grow out and just wear cornrows now," says Mr. Isaac, sending the entire barbershop into fits of laughter.

"Awe, hon, I know you couldn't have messed him up that bad," sighs Sydney, defending her man.

"Nah, I'm just joking. Nathaniel did a wonderful job. It was many years later that I decided to grow my hair out," professes Mr. Isaac. "I had to try to give this ol' cat a splash of hip hop."

Laughter breaks out in the barbershop all over again.

"Real talk, little man," adds Bryan, "Around the barbershop it's kind of a right of passage that the first head your clippers touch on a pro-tip is your mentor's. As a matter of fact, my first paying customer as a professional was your father. And yep, you guessed it, I was nervous as all get out."

Slowly it began to dawn on Nathan he was not alone in his insecurities. He was not alone in crowded New York and most importantly he was not alone in the coming of his manhood. Here in his presence was three great men who had been where he was, had gone through the trials he was facing and had come out on top. He felt blessed and rejuvenated.

The chime of the barbershop door opening coaches Nate from his boyhood contemplation and in walks Chaz.

"What the heck are you doing here?"

"What up, Chaz?" asks Bryan.

Chaz nods never lifting up hooded head to make eye contact but doesn't break stride heading straight towards Nathaniel.

"Whoa, Chaz knows Bryan and my dad?"

Nate watches as Chaz and his father exchange a few inaudible words.

"Bryan, do me a favor and service my customers. I'm going to be tied up for a while," says Nathaniel, escorting Chaz into his office.

"No problem, Boss Man. I got you, just take care of my peeps right there."

Curiosity engulfed Nathan like an alcohol towelette in an open flame. Questions raced through his mind at warp speed. *Why did Bryan call Chaz family? Are they really related?* Boy was Nate glad he has never said anything crass about Chaz to B. *How did Chaz know Nathaniel? What in the world could he and Chaz have to talk about that was going to take a while? Was Chaz there to tell Nathaniel about the run-in that took place at the Minute Mart or was the woodworm blabbing about Nate hanging out with Raw and War?* So many questions, but absolutely no answers.

"Nathan, I'm leaving now," says Sydney, grabbing her large tote bag. "Would you like a ride home?"

What I would like is to know what is going on around here. It's like being in the Twilight Zone, Nate the Great sasses in his mind.

"Think fast. There's no telling how long your dad is going to be in there and the barbershop will be closing in half an hour."

Sydney had made a valid point. Why would he stick around the barbershop and wait while Chaz ratted him out. With the shop closed, there would be no witnesses to keep Nathaniel from grading his behind.

"I'm right behind you, Syd. See you guys tomorrow," Nate says, following Sydney to the exit.

Nathan couldn't get Chaz out of his mind. He wondered if Sydney knew what was up with the woodworm. *"There's only one way to find out,"* he thinks.

Taking a deep breath, Nate bluntly asks Syd what she knew. She was little help, though. All she knew was Chaz was one of the kids from the youth center Nathaniel counseled.

"Makes sense," Nate the Great tells himself. *"Chaz is weird and crazy, definitely a good candidate for counseling."*

"Syd, do you know what my dad is counseling Chaz for . . . about?"

"I sure don't. Your father takes his duties as a counselor very serious. He would never betray the trust of those who pour their hearts out to him in confidence."

"Dad really likes helping people," smiles Nate, proud of his father.

"Yeah Nathan, your dad is a very special man. He really has a way with the wounded. Come on, let me walk you to your building," says Sydney, putting an anti-thief bar on her car's steering wheel.

"I don't need a chaperone," he smarts off mentally.

As they approach the security gate, Nathan realizes Mr. Dan is on duty.

"Hi Mr. Dan. How are you this evening," inquires Sydney courteously.

"I'd be better if I looked half as good as you do."

"Awe, Mr. Dan, that's a sweet thing to say. I see why Mrs. Cora took you off the market all those years ago," blushes Syd.

The grin glides right off Mr. Dan's face the second he realizes Sydney is accompanied by Nathan.

"Boy, when are you going to bring my potholders back? Those were our good potholders!" he snaps harshly.

"I'll take them to Mrs. Cora as soon as I can get in the apartment and put my hands on them," says Nate, walking pass Sydney, not wanting to face grudge-holding Mr. Dan a moment longer than he had to.

Sydney power walks to catch up with Nathan. "You make it your business to get those potholders to Cora tonight. Whoever would have guessed Mr. Dan takes his dish accessories so serious. Maybe we should buy him a few new ones as a peace offering."

"Mrs. Cora said he's just mad because his doctor says he can't have any sweets."

"Well maybe we should buy him some sugar free candy then," giggles Syd.

"Maybe we should," laughs Nate.

"Goodnight Nathan. I'll call you in a little while to make sure you are alright."

"Okay Sydney, but give me time to run the potholders up the hall."

"No problem," Sydney replies, disappearing into the darkness headed towards apartment building 2, in which she lived.

Inside the apartment he and his father share, Nathan drops his backpack in the middle of the floor and v-lines for the frig. He stands there with the refrigerator door open, looking for a snack and drinking orange juice straight from the cartoon.

"Nathan, you 'no better than standing there with the frigerator open like that. You gon' run up your daddy's light bill," he imagines Ola Mae saying.

Smiling from ear to ear, he paws an apple and closes the refrigerator door, "I hear you, Me'ma. Love you much . . . miss you more."

A glimmer of red catches his eye, "Potholders!" he exclaims. "Let me take these worn out old thangs back to their owner before Mr. Dan takes us on People's Court," he smirks, throwing the potholders in a plastic grocery bag.

Nathan delivered the potholders to the Dan residence and while he was there, Cora filled him up with chocolate chip cookies she had been hiding from her husband. Her kindness almost made him feel bad about the way he spoke to Mr. Dan, *almost.*

"I hate to eat and run, Mrs. Cora, but I have to get back home. Dad is working late counseling and Sydney is going to call any time now to check on me."

"I understand. If you have missed her call, I'll gladly vouch for you, as long as you keep our cookie crunching a secret."

"Deal. Goodnight."

"Goodnight," she says, dead bolting the door behind him.

"Psk! Psk!" echoes from the shadow of the hallway.

Instantly, survival instincts kick in and Nathan analyzes his options, flight or fight.

"Don't be alarmed young-buck. It's only me, Knick Nate," declares J-ran, emerging from the dimly lit corner.

"Oh, J-ran, man you almost took me back to my scrapping days," says Nate, hoping Jyran believed his tough-guy front.

"Be easy, little man. Put your fist away. I come in peace."

"Cool," replies Nate, wondering what would bring J-ran inside the apartment complex. It is common knowledge the Heights Knights are not warmly welcomed on the premises.

"Raw and War are highly pissed off with you. They said you ain't got heart and for sure you ain't Knight material. But I think they're mistaken."

"Mr. J-ran they-"

Jyran cuts Nathan off with the wave of his index finger from the right of his own jaw line to the left without actually touching his skin. "What'd I tell you, Knick Nate? Call me J-ran, all my friends do and you are my *friend*, right?"

Jyran closes the gap between him and Nathan.

"Yeah, we are friends J-ran," declares Nate. "I was just going to say that Raw and War misunderstood the other day, that's all."

"That's easy to do."

"Yeah. See my old friend from Georgia was visiting and *they* had words. Max thinks he's better than everybody and he kind of instigated some mess with the twins. I just tried to keep down the confusion," exaggerates Nate the Great, making Max out to be a villain.

"It's cool, Knick Nate. You don't owe me no explanation. As long as you stay loyal and don't cross me, we are always going to be cool," he grins deceitfully. "In fact, I don't usually do this because I don't really run with the young-bucks. I usually let some of the cats under me handle recruits. But I see something special in you and felt the need to oversee your initiation personally."

Nathan's chest begins to swell with pride, *"J-ran, head of the Heights Knights, thinks I'm somebody, somebody special. Sweet!"* he gloats to himself.

"What do I have to do?" Nate asks eagerly.

"See, that's exactly what I love about you," chuckles J-ran, patting Nathan on the back, "you're always down for whatever. You're my kind of man! The kind that would be a great asset to my crew."

"I tried to get Raw and War to see that," boasts Nate.

"Knick Nate, bump what Raw and War think . . . they think what *I* tell them to think. In fact, don't even worry yourself with them. Leave the terrible two to me. I came by here to give you the game plan for your official initiation."

Jyran pauses to make sure he has Nathan's undivided attention. Sure enough, he does.

"I'm all ears."

"Check it, remember your beef with that chump Chaz?"

Nate the Great nods, yes.

"Well, here's what you have to do . . ."

Nathan's eyes light up with deviousness, as malicious strategy dances off Jyran's tongue and into his ear.

"You think you can handle that?" asks J-ran.

"It would be my pleasure," insists Nate, beyond confident.

"Me and the twins will meet you there."

"Cool."

"I'ma get up out of here now," says Jyran, looking at his expensive watch.

"Until tomorrow," mutters Nate, as Jyran jogs up the hall and into Sydney.

"Move trick," declares J-ran, shoving her a little.

"Busted," thinks Nathan.

"What is he doing in here? Is he in here to see you? Were you talking to him? What did I tell you, Nathan? We had an understanding, didn't we?" she says, finally ending her many interrogation questions without ever giving Nate the opportunity to respond.

Sydney grabs Nathan's hand but he snatches it away. "Boy, have you lost your ever-loving mind? Trust me, you'd rather deal with me than your father, and so help me God I will tell Nathaniel everything!"

"You're not going to be pulling on me all kinds of way just because you're mad. I know what it looks like, but it's not what you think," he yells cunningly.

Mrs. Cora opens her apartment door after looking out the peephole. "Is everything alright out here?" she asks.

"Everything is fine, Cora. I was just escorting Nathan home," replies Sydney, attempting to mask her anger.

"My word," sighs Mrs. Cora. "This is all my fault. Nathan told me he had to be getting on back home but I convinced him to stay a while and have a few cookies. I hate eating alone and Joseph can't have sweets. I was just trying to kill two birds with one stone . . . avoiding having dessert alone and keeping from tempting my Joe from sneaking a chocolate chip. I didn't mean to get Nathan in trouble. Don't be mad at him, Syd. It truly is my fault he was not home when you called," pleads Cora.

"I told you it wasn't what you thought," hollers Nathan, storming off.

"Thanks for clearing things up," sighs Sydney embarrassed.

"Sorry," Mrs. Cora apologizes again.

"Nathan, wait up," Syd calls out, giving chase.

"What do you want to yell at me about now?" he asks, holding the door of his father's apartment almost closed so that Sydney cannot enter.

"Look Nathan, everybody makes mistakes and I apologize. I became so enraged when I saw Jyran I was irrational. I jumped to conclusions before getting all the details." Sydney exhales noisily and leans up against the hallway wall. "One day when you have kids you'll understand."

Nathan opens the door wide and glares dead in her eyes. "Just a reminder, Syd, *you* don't have kids. *My* mother is *dead*, in case you forgot, and you are a piss-poor substitute!" he declares fiercely and slams the door.

"The boy has a point," Sydney enlightens herself. *"How am I going to explain this to Nathaniel?"* she thinks, lightly banging her head on the wall. *"Maybe I should back off. I get the feeling Nathan is feeling a bit threatened."*

Sydney vanished into the badly lit courtyard headed home, her mind made up to give Nathan and Nathaniel some space to nurture their newly forming father-son union. After all, just as Nate said, she was not family.

CHAPTER SEVEN

Wood Wonderland Workshop

The next morning came far too soon for Nathan. He'd had a very restless night and hadn't gotten much sleep at all. He didn't know if it was his conscience catching up with him or what. Ola Mae had always told him the soul couldn't rest properly if it was being haunted by bad acts. Disrespect . . . lying . . . plotting the downfall of woodworms, Nate was sure all of those things were unmistakably bad acts.

"Rise and shine, my little lumber jack," says Nathaniel, introducing light to Nathan's room.

"I'm up . . . I'm up." Slowly Nate unwraps his puny body from the sheets. Apparently Syd hadn't uttered a word to his father about their encounter.

"I can't tell, sleepyhead. I thought we'd hail a cab and get a bite to eat in the diner a couple blocks away. You know, start your big day off right."

"Sounds good to me," Nate whispers, trying to muster some pep.

"Well, get a move on. You still have to get to school afterwards."

"I'll be ready in twenty. Is Sydney coming with us?"

"No Sidekick, it's just going to be you and me. Why do you think I said we are going to hail a cab? Twenty minutes," bellows Nathaniel, closing Nathan's room door behind him.

Forty minutes later in a quaint diner across from Simon's bagel stand Nate finds himself blankly staring at his dad.

"What's on your mind, son? You're not eating your food. You're just stirring in it."

"Nothing . . . I . . . I, nothing," Nate stammers, unsure what to say or how to say it.

His father blows then quietly sips his coffee, giving Nathan time to get his thoughts together. However, he soon realizes he'll be waiting forever for Nate to further their conversation.

"Sidekick, I promised you we could talk about any and everything. I can't help you if I don't know what your problem is."

But silence has a stronghold on Nate's yearning to vent.

"Is this about your presentation this evening?" inquires Nathaniel, a slim trace of irritation from his son's muteness.

Nathan nods deceitfully.

"Trust me, Nathan Campbell, you are going to be just fine. Facing your fears strips them of their power."

"I'm not . . . I hear you, dad."

"Good. You may not have your Me'ma here with you physically, but she and your mama are watching you from heaven, protecting you. And never forget you have a strong support system right here to tap into any time . . . there's the Andrew's, Isaac, Bryan, Sydney, and me. You even have the Dans in your corner. Between the flock of us, we should be able to conquer anything that comes up."

True, Nathan recognizes he had supporters both in Georgia and New York. However, the Dan's, well at least one of them, was on the 'maybe' list of allies along with Sydney. The sheer thought of Ola Mae and Abigail watching over him rattles Nate clear to the bone. He was sure neither would be remotely happy with his unruly behavior.

"Don't worry about me, dad. It is just my nerves trying to get the best of me. I'm sure I'll be just fine when I look out into the crowd and see you and the rest of the barbershop crew cheering me on."

"That's my son! Now let's get you off to school, Sidekick."

The majority of Nathan's school day was spent preparing for the Wood Wonderland workshop. In fact, all the students actively participating in the workshop were excused from their regular classes in order to help set everything up. As Nate looked around the auditorium, he was mesmerized. The Wonderland Workshop housed many different categories: Woodland Creatures, Garden Escape Arena, Group Goodies, Miscellaneous and Home 'Works' which consist of crafty wooden home decor.

The students of Hill Street Academy had worked wood

masterpieces. No two pieces were even the least bit similar. There was abstract art that could blend in seamlessly in a professional gallery. There were woodland creatures, sculpted cute bunnies, fat frumpy frogs, cuddly teddy bears and squirrels. Many were welcome statues or yard ornaments. But the most impressive carved sculpture had to be a ferocious timber wolf, clearly the work of an advanced student. Nate really appreciated the way Mr. Fields had selected the best of each skill group to be put on display. It showed parents and other students the possible growth.

"Mr. Nathan Campbell," calls out Mr. Fields. "I need to speak to you."

"Sure, just give me a second to drop this window-box off over there at the Garden Escape Arena."

"Okay. I'll be slurping up some cold water at the water fountain," says the shop teacher, wiping sweat from his bush brow.

"What could this be about?" Nate quizzes himself, setting down the heavy but beautiful window box.

A large black canvas catches Nathan's eye. Nosiness takes him by the hand and leads him to the structure.

"I wouldn't do that if I were you," a plump, freckled face redhead boy says, hiding behind a makeshift tool shed, eating a Snickers candy bar.

"Mind your own business, Chucky," Nate barks, placing the hand he was about to use to unveil the canvas's contents in his pocket.

"I'm just saying . . ." Chucky says, smacking on the gooey chocolate.

"You were just saying nothing, fat fart. You too busy feeding your obese face."

"Okay, go ahead and peep at Chaz's project and see won't Mr. Fields kick you out of the workshop," cautions Chucky, surfacing from his hiding spot. "Don't say I didn't try to warn you, freakazoid!"

"Shut up!" growls Nathan, searching the vicinity for their teacher.

Mr. Fields makes eye contact and waves Nate towards him.

"Chaz . . . Chaz . . . Chaz—dear sweet woodworm gets to make a special presentation," he jeers jealously.

"I just wanted to commend you, Nathan, for your work. I mean, you picked up techniques and crafts two and three-year shop students still can't grasp," brags Mr. Fields.

"Thank you a lot," replies Nate, yet to become comfortable excepting compliments.

"Don't thank me. You are the one who possesses God-given talent. I was going to surprise you but it's eating me up. I've never been good at keeping secrets."

Suspense closes in on Nate like a hungry lion. *"What is it . . . spit it out please,"* begs Nathan's interior.

"We are going to honor you with a plaque of achievement," declares Mr. Fields, well pleased. "You are the very first first-year woodshop student to ever be featured in the Wood Wonderland Workshop. Let me be the first to congratulate you."

"I don't know what to say," Nate sighs, dumbfounded, " . . . thanks."

"You earned it. Wear something extra nice. Your picture is bound to end up in the Hill Street Academy Gazette."

Nathan was overwhelmed. *"Wow,"* he thought, *"me in a newspaper for winning an award."* Nate was truly astonished by the idea. His fourth grade teacher once told him he'd make headline news one day, with a caption reading 'America's most wanted.' Nathan wondered if Mrs. Higginbottom still works at Doversville Middle School. He'd have to send Max a copy to rub in her face.

"Ah, Max," exhales Nate, dismayed by a heavy conscience. *"A fence I need to mend. The Andrews were incredibly kind to me."*

At the close of the school day, the woodshop students had the auditorium in tiptop shape. It was the ultimate in lumber luxury. The exhibits were so stunning, termites would starve themselves to death before daring to munch on anything displayed. Nathan felt magnificent. For once in his life he was apart of something great, him and him alone. There was no Max, no Maxwell and Mary Andrews, no Ola Mae, and no Nathaniel. He had created this great work solo. No one had held his hand.

"Good afternoon, Sal," Nate says, hopping inside the cab.

"Good afternoon it is indeed. I'm happy to see you are in a chipper mood for a change."

"Yep, today has been one of the best days of my life. I didn't have to go to not one class today. I spent the whole day helping fix up the auditorium. Then tonight it gets even better. I am going to get an award during the workshop," gloats Nate.

"And after that, the icing on the cake. I'm going to get Chaz and become a Heights Knight," he says silently.

"An award? Congratulations! Your father must be so proud of you, Nathan!" exclaims Sal.

"He doesn't know yet. I just found out a couple hours ago myself. I think I'm going to let it be a surprise. What do you think, Sal?"

"I think that is one of the best surprises a father could ever get."

"Good. I'll let you know how it goes Monday."

"Please do. See you next week, Nathan," says Sal, pulling up to Clipper Creations.

"Speaking of the man of the hour," declares Bryan, "Come on over here and let me touch up your tape. We can't have you looking shabby for your big night."

"True, but my presentation is so gorgeous it'll make me look good if I was wearing high-waters, suspenders and thick grandpa bifocals," brags Nate, plopping down in Bryan's chair.

"I like your confidence, Nathan. Believing in yourself is half the battle," announces Mr. Isaac.

"Mr. Isaac and Bryan are both right. You need inner and outer confidence. Your outside should reflect your inside. So when you are finished getting your hair cut, we are leaving early. I had Mrs. Cora go pick up a few new threads for you. I wanted you to look your best for your woodworking debut," proclaims Nathaniel, excited.

"Hill Street should have workshops more often. Bryan hooking up my cut, Mr. Isaac passing out compliments, and Dad buying me new clothes, I don't know how to act," clowns Nate, making everyone laugh.

"Hey Sidekick, when you are well behaved and show you're doing something honest and positive with your time, you find great favor with others. People don't think twice about showing you love in words and deeds."

"I gotta keep that in mind," replies Nate.

"I have to admit Nathan, I'm actually excited about tonight," confides Mr. Isaac. "It takes an awful lot to make an old cat like me leave the house after dark. You must be real special."

"Yeah, little dude, I can't wait either. Your boy B is ready to cheer you on," adds Bryan.

Sydney continues to quietly braid her client's hair as if she is not following the conversation. Although he hopes her answer is no, Nathan asks anyway, "What about you, Syd? Are you coming tonight too?"

She doesn't even glance up, "Would you like me to?"

"Why did she have to go there? Why couldn't she just have said no"? Nate nonverbally inquires of his conscience? *"She knows I can't say 'heck nah, I don't want you there, mommy-wanna-be.' Dad would skin my hindquarters."*

"I guess . . . I mean if you don't already have plans," Nathan responds dryly.

"We can all take my car if ya'll want to. I'm sure the five of us can easily fit. This way no one has to a pay cab fair," Sydney suggests, her way of accepting Nathan's insincere invitation.

"That sounds good to me," says Mr. Isaac. "In fact, I won't even go home after work. I have an extra set of clothes in the back, back there. I'll just cop a squat at your place, Syd, if you don't mind. That goes for you too, Nathaniel. I respect what you and Sydney have going on and I'd never dare want to step on your toes."

"Oh no, Mr. Isaac, I don't have a problem with that at all. I know you have come to love Syd like a daughter," says Nathaniel, brushing loose clipper shavings off Nathan and ushering him out the barbershop door.

"Nathan is turning into a mighty impressive young man," states Mr. Isaac to Bryan, nodding in approval.

"Man, dad, Mrs. Cora has some real good taste. I gotta admit I was kind of scared of what might be waiting for me here. I don't mean no harm, but Mr. Dan be wearing some ugly clothes and I just thought Mrs. Cora was the one doing the shopping," says Nate at home in his room.

"Nathan, you are a mess. What am I going to do with you," chuckles his father.

"You know I'm right. Men don't like shopping and their women usually buy their clothes."

"Oh Sidekick, I didn't say you didn't have a valid point. I just said you are a mess."

"I'm going to wear the soft yellow shirt, the navy blue pants and the blue and yellow tie."

"Excellent choice," declares Nathaniel, surprised by his son's selections. "Sydney and Mr. Isaac will be here soon. Chop! Chop!"

"Why did he mention Sydney?" Nate asks himself.

In the beginning Nathan had been smitten with her. But since he was so young and he was sure there would be many other girls in his life, he stepped aside and welcomed the relationship between Syd and his father. The purpose was to make his father happy. However, lately Sydney was becoming nothing more than a sharp pain in Nathan's neck. Her sheer presence was starting to annoy him. He felt she was too nosey, always at the wrong place at the wrong time. And that place just happens to be in Nate the Great's business. He had to come up with a plan to break them up.

Sydney and Mr. Isaac arrives bearing ice cream. The simple knowledge the sweet treat came from Syd is enough to turn Nathan's stomach. "None for me, thanks. I'm already kinda nervous. Combine that with dairy products and I'll probably end up with the bubble-guts or chucking cream."

"Sidekick!" proclaims Nathaniel, shocked by his son's descriptive choice of words. "Too much information."

"Well, I'll just put yours in the freezer for later, handsome," grins Sydney.

"Syd is right, Nathan you are looking like crisp new money," agrees Mr. Isaac. "That pale yellow looks good against your dark skin."

"Sweetness, will you do me a favor," asks Nathaniel, handing Sydney a digital camera. "Take a picture of me, Nathan and Mr. Isaac."

"It'll be my pleasure."

Nathaniel, Nathan and Mr. Isaac pose for the photograph. *"Mr.*

Isaac is probably the closest I'm ever going to get to a grandpa," thinks Nate, heavy laden.

He hadn't given grandfathers much mind play. His life had been filled with strong women, Ola Mae and then Eva, Mary and Suzann. Even little Olivia had been strong-willed. Dr. Andrews was more of a confidant to him than father figure.

Truth be told Nate, was taken back by living with his father. It had been many months now and he really longed for a motherly touch, not Sydney though. Now he found himself wishing the only living link to his mother, his Grandpa Jackson, would put his personal feelings for Nathaniel aside and reach out to him.

"We men got to stick together," his ego rings out.

As soon as he got rid of Syd, he was going to try to be the blood bridge between his dad and his mother's father.

"Now let's get one of the dynamic father and son duo. Then one of Nathaniel and Mr. Isaac and then one of Nathan and Mr. Isaac," dictates Sydney.

"And after all that how about you show me how to use that fancy camera so you can get in a picture or two," proposes Mr. Isaac.

"How sweet of you," chimes Syd.

"Let's make it quick ya'll. We have to get to the school soon."

Just as Nathaniel, Nathan and Mr. Isaac conclude their photo session, there's a rat-tat-tat on the apartment door.

"Yo! It's B! I know ya'll didn't leave without me," Bryan says, attempting to see in the peephole.

"Get your silly self on in here, boy," declares Mr. Isaac, opening the door.

"What can I say, besides I'm fashionably late," smirks Bryan, spinning around like Michael Jackson.

And fashionable he was indeed. Nathan couldn't recall ever seeing anyone so sharp, as Ola Mae would say. Byran was sporting some pure movie star gear. He seemed to have stepped right off the cover of GQ magazine.

"B! You are just in time to take a picture with us," demands Nate, clutching hold of Bryan's hand and pulling him right between him and Sydney.

"For sho dude. Syd, you gonna have to make several copies of these bad boys," declares Bryan, taking a picture perfect stance.

"Quickly, Mr. Isaac," pleads Nathaniel. "We have to hit the road."

The streets leading to Hill Street Academy were littered with people and cars. Nate the Great hadn't expected such a huge turnout. Suddenly the butterflies in his stomach transform into pterodactyls. The thought of having the spotlight shone on him while receiving his award was wreaking havoc on Nathan's insides. His palms and pits were drenched.

"You alright, young-buck?" asked B, sensing the change in Nate's demeanor as they walk through the endless rows of cars to get to the auditorium.

"Yeah, I'm good."

"With God, all things are possible . . . you can do all things through Christ which strengthens you . . . this included," whispers Nathaniel to his son.

"Right! Thanks, Superhero."

"No, thank you for being an even better son than I ever dreamed possible."

Whoa! Nathaniel's statement was so deep and emotion driven, Nate the Great staggered in drunkenness. His father thought *he* was great. There Nathan was thinking he was a disappointment to his father and family's name. After all, he had been nothing but trouble since the day he was born. No matter what anyone had ever said, Nathan blamed himself for his mother's untimely death. He secretly cried in bed late at night consumed by guilt, murmuring under his breath, *"If I was never born, she would still be alive. She would have never died."*

How could he deface his father's title for him with violent gang activity? It was apparent the mighty Nate the Great had some big boy decisions to make. Nevertheless, another storm had begun brewing. Nathan had never deemed himself the smartest person in the world, but somehow he knew getting out of a gang initiation would not be easy. In fact, it could very well prove to be downright dangerous.

"Hi Nathan," yells his shop teacher over the faint roar of the crowded auditorium.

"Hey, Mr. Fields. I'd like you to meet my father, Nathaniel, Mr.

Isaac the wisest mentor, Bryan the hippest barber in New York, and Sydney."

"Nice to meet you folks. Hope you enjoy our little workshop," says Mr. Fields, shaking the hand of everyone Nate introduced to him.

"This is amazing," awes Sydney. "Did students really do all of this?"

"They sure did."

"Only because we have the very best shop teacher in the world," replies Nathan.

Mr. Fields blushes, "I don't know about all that. I just love wood and working with it."

"Well, Mr. Fields, I can tell you this much. Your love for wood has definitely rubbed off on my son," says Nathaniel.

"I admit it, Mr. Campbell, Nathan is as natural as raw knotted pine," declares the tubby teacher. "Your boy has timber talent."

"I can't wait to see his talent in 3D."

"Speaking of your work, Nathan, it's time for you to relieve Chucky at your station. You folks may want to mingle so you can sneak a peek at everything the Wood Wonderland Workshop has to offer. Our official presentations will begin in about thirty minutes."

"Nathan, we are going to walk around and check out some things. We'll catch up with you in a bit, okay."

"Okay."

Nathaniel, Sydney, Bryan and Mr. Isaac disappeared in one direction and Nathan followed Mr. Fields in another. The closer they got to Nate's station, the roaring waves in his tummy began to subside and comfort for his craft took center stage.

"Bout time you showed up," snaps Chucky, taking off the workshop apron and tossing it at Nathan. "I'm about to starve to death."

"Like you need something to eat," snickers Nate softly.

Mr. Fields sticks around for a few to watch Nathan in action. Nate works the crowd interested in his assigned workstation like Bob Villa. He wows the bystanders with his knowledge of wood and the techniques used to create the things showcased. Mr. Isaac watches from the back of the crowd, pleased that the rough-around-the-edges son of his prized pupil was coming into his own—finally appearing to be at home in his own skin. The thirty minutes until show time elapsed rapidly.

"Uhm . . . Uhm," says Mr. Fields on the stage platform, tapping the microphone. "Ladies and gentlemen, can I have your attention please? It's time to start our assembly. I have to tell you all, I am very happy with this year's Wood Wonderland Workshop. The students here at Hill Street Academy have put on their thinking caps and made masterpieces, as you will see.

I am grateful to be a part of this great event. The kids here have put their hearts and souls into each piece you have seen tonight. Believe it or not, one of the more outstanding craftsmen featured tonight is a first year student."

Nate's heart drops into the pit of his gut because he knows where Mr. Fields is going with his speech.

The shop instructor continues, "This student is not only new at wood work, he is new to our fair city. He was taken under the wing of my most valued protégé, and he instantly caught on."

Nathan's eyes dance across the swarm of people. For the first time since arriving at the Wonderland Wood Workshop his thoughts rest on Chaz. But his archenemy was nowhere to be found, not even at the presentation site. There was an enchanting girl bobbing in and out from behind the canvas covering Chaz's surprise.

Nate had never seen the mysterious girl before. She was breathtaking. Her hair was long and silky. It wrapped around her face like a shiny black frame. Her skin was as light as a batch of banana nut bread muffins Eva had once baked for Nate and she had the deepest dimples he had ever seen.

"Daaang!" he tells himself, popping his collar and adjusting his tie.

The young girl was hot, to say the least. She was dressed like a Keke Palmer doll, dark blue skinny jeans and a soft almost sheer black ruffled, flare-tailed, loose-fit halter top. The mystery model's top was v-neck, but revealed nothing but a nice sized diamond studded butterfly pendant that draped elegantly from an almost invisibly thin rope chain. To top it all off, she was rocking black Nike tennis shoes, just the hint of tomboy that made her even more appealing to Nathan.

"That figures," Nate the Great grumbles. *"A dork like Chaz would have a beautiful girl on his arm, and the fool doesn't even have the decency to help her set up his presentation."*

Mr. Fields continues on, "At this time, the ushers are walking around selling raffle tickets for one dollar. Your generous donations will be used to help with the renovation of Hill Street Academy. The lucky person whose name is pulled from our ticket pool will win Chaz's contribution to this year's Wonderland Workshop. Trust me everyone, as you will soon see, it is well worth the dollar donation."

"If they were auctioning off Chaz's date, I'd put up all the money I'll make in a year at the barbershop," salivates Nate.

"But before we get to the raffle, Hill Street Academy and I would like to honor a very special student. He's new but deserves recognition for his wood working ability. I've seen many of you drooling over the traditional grandfather clock located in our Home Works station. Believe it or not, that clock was made by a new pulp pupil," chuckles Mr. Fields alone, no one else is amused by his pun. "Ahem . . . anyhow, without further ado, I would like to present this achievement award to Nathan Campbell."

The crowd begins thunderous applause and Nathaniel bear hugs his son in sheer pride. "Why didn't you tell me, Sidekick?"

"I wanted it to be a surprise," responds Nate, teary-eyed.

"Com' on up here, Nathan, and accept your award!"

"I'm so proud of you. Go on and get your plaque!" demands Nathaniel.

Nervously, Nate climbs the steps onto the stage.

"Would you like to say a few words?" asks Mr. Fields.

"Uhmm . . ." stammers Nate, "I just want to say thank you, that's all."

"Not a man of many words," smiles Ms. Carol, "but definitely a young man of great talent!" She, Mr. Fields, and Nathan yield to the flash of cameras. "Congratulations again, Nathan."

Nathan nods, flabbergasted by his mini celebrity status and descends the stage. Finding himself smothered by the delight of his makeshift family, Nathaniel, Mr. Isaac, Bryan and Sydney.

"You gon' have to beat the ladies off you now," exclaims Bryan, giving Nate a pound.

Instantly Nathan thinks of one cutie in particular he'd like to have take great interest in him, little miss mystery at Chaz's station. To his surprise even she was applauding his success.

"Okay parents, faculty, students and prestigious guests, we are going to keep the program moving right along. Mayor O'Connell, if you would join us up here, we'd like you to have the pleasure of pulling the winning name from out of the ticket pool," announces Ms. Carol. As the rather young looking mayor takes his place at the podium, the ushers collect last minute entries.

"While we are waiting on the ushers, let's have a look at the prize up for grabs. If you would unveil the timber treasure," Mr. Fields calls out, as he points to the girl standing at Chaz's presentation.

Beauty rips the tarp off Chaz's handy-work with the skill of one of the Price is Right babes. Embarrassed, Nate the Great is dazed by his enemy's design.

Chaz had proven to be the ultimate wood craftsmen. Mr. Fields explained how Chaz spent numerous hours before and after school working diligently on the bench swing and its base. Nate knew it took weeks just to chisel and grout the detail into the swing's backrest and canopy. He looked around, the gleam in the eyes of his father no longer belonged to him. Rage grows within him like an oxygen-enveloped fire.

"This buster has taken it too far. My own dad is slobbering over 'em. How quickly we forget! Thanks a lot, dad," simmered Nate the Great. *"I'ma make you pay Chaz, in blood!"*

"That's a real nice swing," sighs Sydney, "Too bad we really don't have any place to put it.

"Who asked you?" thinks Nate furious.

"What you mean you don't have anywhere to put it. You all have that large virtually empty courtyard in the Heights."

"Mr. Isaac, can you imagine the fights and disarray that lovely swing would cause. All the tenants would be at each other's throats over it," giggles Sydney.

"You have a point there. Hadn't thought about it like that. Too bad."

"I guess if I win I could always send it to Eva," interjects Nathaniel. "She'd put it to good use. Wouldn't she, Sidekick?"

Nate forges a fake smile. "She sure would," he replies, all the while envisioning himself tearing Chaz's swing to shreds.

"Okay, our ushers have just informed us they have collected all donations and ticket stubs." Ms. Carol holds up one finger to the crowd and covers the microphone as another staff member whispers in her ear. "Ladies and gentlemen, it is my great pleasure to announce during the course of this month-long raffle and including the estimated proceeds from tonight, the Wood Wonderland Workshop has raised nine thousand, seven hundred, and forty one dollars."

Deafening praise saturates the auditorium.

"Now, Mayor O'Connell, if you would select the winner of that fabulous swing," insists the assistant principal, stirring the ticket stubs in a large decorative box.

"I hope I'm not disqualified because I'm drawing from the ticket pool," declares the mayor. "There's a spot in my back yard that has that swing's name written all over it."

The crowd laughs briefly. Anticipation is thick.

"Drum-roll please," says Ms. Carol, signaling the band.

Mayor O'Connell clears his throat, "The winner is Nathaniel Campbell, owner of Clipper Creations Barbershop!"

"Great!" utters Nathan.

"Mr. Campbell please join us over at the swing for a picture or two," demands Ms. Carol.

Nathaniel promises he won't be long and leaves Nate in the care of Sydney.

"Syd, where did Bryan and Mr. Isaac slip off to?" he asks, not wishing to be left alone with her.

"They are headed over to the annual candlelight vigil in the parking lot of St. Matthew's. You know the huge church at the intersection of Fifth and Main. They attend it every year."

"What's a vigil?" inquires Nate the Great.

"Umm, well a vigil is like a memorial for lost love ones. The one at St. Matthew's honors the victims of gang violence."

"Who did Bryan and Mr. Isaac lose to gang violence?"

"It's a long story, Nathan, and now really isn't the time to talk about it," says Sydney, shrugging off his question.

During the course of their conversation, Nate loses track of his father and Chaz's chick posing with the group at the swing.

"Where did my dad go? I don't see him in the crowd," proclaims Nathan, irritated with Sydney's presence.

"He's probably giving Chaz a few words of encouragement. She's supposed to address the spectators at the vigil tonight."

"Chaz speaking at the vigil . . . that's funny since he was about a half hour from becoming a victim to gang violence," retorts Nate in his head.

"Whoa, Syd did you say *she?*" asked Nathan, his thoughts finally processing the fullness of Sydney's statement.

"Yeah, Chaz is short for Chastity. I thought you knew, after all ya'll do go to the same school."

There was no way Nathan was going to ambush a girl! He had to stop J-ran and the Heights Knights. It was all beginning to make sense. J-ran knew Chaz was a girl and just didn't care. He knew she would be speaking at the vigil and had set up the attack for afterwards so the gang could escape under the cover of darkness and blend in with the crowd of partakers.

Why dids Chaz dress the way she did? Was she ashamed of being a girl?

"I gotta go!" yells Nate, dashing for the door.

"Nathan! Nathan! Come back!" Sydney calls out after him. "Nathaniel is going to kill me! How can I lose a thirteen year old?" she sighs.

CHAPTER EIGHT

Battle worth fighting?

Nathan's mind and feet seemed to be in some sort of contest, each trying to out-race the other. He runs with speed and purpose. Nate the Great had always fashioned himself a thug by nature, but beating up on females in his opinion was a punk move. He would never stoop that low. His Me'ma branded upon his brain that he should treat all females like he would want people to treat her, and there was absolutely no way he would ever want *anybody* jumping on his grandmother.

As he rounds the corner of Main Street, his feet shift from third gear to neutral and he coasts up to the back of the seamless crowd. "Now what?" he whispers to himself.

"Blend in," common sense speaks back to him, *"Blend in and take in your surroundings. Locate all targets, J-ran, Raw, War and Chaz while avoiding Mr. Isaac and Bryan."*

Immediately Nathan's eyes pick up where his feet left off. He easily spots Chaz. She is standing on the platform, waiting her turn to address the crowd. Bryan and Mr. Isaac are at the base of the platform stage, second only to security. J-ran, Raw and War, Nate knows are incognito.

This was a vigil against gang violence. Naturally, gang members would not boldly draw attention to themselves. Security and the police were everywhere. The Heights Knights and any other gang would be fools to spotlight themselves.

"Maybe I won't have to do anything," Nate's core echoes. "With heat in full force, maybe I can convince J-ran to postpone my initiation. Then I'll just avoid the Heights Knights until they get the picture."

"Sounds like you are trying to go out like some pissy pants pansy," growls Nate the Great, challenging Nathan's conscience.

"You wanna be known as a sissy? The tough streets of New York ain't no place for crybabies."
Ola Mae's words softly resound in Nathan's head, *"Treat females how you want people to treat ya Me'ma, baby."*
He couldn't go against the training of Ola Mae, not on this subject any way. Nathan knew he had been very disobedient and defied, even deceived his grandmother at times, but this was entirely different. He knew if he attempts to carry out J-ran's initiation, every time he drew back to strike Chaz he would see Ola Mae's face. He could never in a million years hit his Me'ma.
The priest speaking had a very monotone voice. It was soothing and Nathan begins to relax. His heart is no longer racing and the cool night breeze is erasing the perspiration from his sprint over.
"I might as well chill out," he tells himself. *"Nothing is going to happen until the vigil is over and if I have to fight the Heights Knights, I'm going to need everything in me. So it'll be smart to rest up and save what energy I have left."*
The hush over the crowd and the shimmer from handheld candles set a sad yet hopeful disposition. People were crying silent tears, each Nate imagined has lost someone to or themselves been a victim of gang violence. Although many were crying with every word Father Brinson spoke, the glimmer of hope shining in their eyes grew. Hope for gang, drug and violence free streets. Hope for healing, hope for brotherly love, hope for peace of mind and serenity.
Countless spectators wear 'in memory of' t-shirts. A few shirts billboard the smiling faces of babies and young children, obviously brought to their innocent ends at the hands of gangs. Was this the life Nathan wants for himself, surely not. Neither did he want to become one of the lifeless smiles captured only on paper and fabric, nor to cause anyone else's face to be memorialized in such a way.
He could kick himself for falling for the hype. Back in Doversville, he had never been a follower. He was always the leader. Yet here in New York, he was letting himself become a funky follower for the sake of a false sense of friendship. Nah, that was a no-hap. J-ran's plan had just backfired.
Having Knick Nate the Great's initiation follow the vigil was the

biggest mistake he could have ever made. Only a cold and heartless person could hurt someone after such an emotional and love driven ceremony, and Nathan had a heart. The fact that it often ached for his lost loved ones and disappointments, and at times was even warmed by kindness and pride, was evidence.

This was a battle worth fighting. If he took a beating from the Knights, so be it. *"If you don't stand for something, you'll fall for anything,"* a wise woman once told him. The message was now clear. Nathan was going to take a stand to defend Chaz. He was going to take a stand on behalf of his Me'ma Ola Mae, his mama Abigail, his foster granny Eva 'the Grandma Diva', on behalf of women and girls everywhere. He had made a conscience decision not to fall for the Heights Knight's hype a second longer.

Where was the glory and honor in acting gangster? Always sneaking around, often times stealing and preying on the helpless or unexpecting. It didn't take a big man to defeat a lesser being. Where was the art in 'taking candy from a baby?' In the glow of white wax and flickering flames, Nate the Great found redemption. An epiphany encased his thought process like a golden halo. Only the insecure found power in bullying and intimidation.

"Now ladies and gentlemen," echoes Father Brinson through the P.A. system. "Please welcome a newcomer to our vigil, Ms. Chastity Davis. I ask that you be patient with her as she shares her testimonial."

Tender applause greets Chaz as she takes her place at the podium. Nathan notices she has changed out of her cute black blouse and into a memorial t-shirt displaying a stunningly beautiful young woman, instantly the photo image of his own mother graces his mind.

"Maybe I can have the picture of my mom put on a shirt too," he thought.

"Ahem," Chaz sighs, taking in a deep breath, "I'm sorry this is more difficult than I thought it would be."

A tall, brown skinned man joins Chaz at the platform and places his hand on her shoulder in support.

"Take your time, baby girl," Bryan calls out from the crowd.

Chaz smiles in the direction of his voice. "Like Father Brinson told you, my name is Chastity Davis. Many of you know me as Chaz.

I'm thirteen years old and last year my older sister Charity was killed during a gang shooting." She pauses to allow the onlookers to gaze at the photo on her shirt. "She was only seventeen years old and as you can see she was gorgeous. Charity was a member of the Heights Knights, queen of the Knights if you may. Little did my sister know her outer beauty could not hold a candle to her inner beauty, she was a queen, period, to my mother and father . . . to me."

Silent streams cuddled Chaz's cheeks as she fought to choke out pain and emotion. Nathan found himself teary eyed and looked towards the heavens in hopes his tears will return back to where they had come. The crowd was hushed, giving Chaz all the time she needed to continue.

Nate's gaze fell upon Bryan. To his amazement, he too was crying. Tough talking, slang spitting, thuggish barber Bryan, crying shamelessly. Once more Nate realized considering crying as a weakness was yet another insecurity.

"The loss of Charity sparked a flame in our community. The people of the Heights united to take a stance against gangs and violence . . . a stand against the Height's Knights. Vowing not to lose any beauty—or brawn, for that matter—to the streets."

J-ran's plan had become even clearer now. Nathan's was just a pawn in his plot for vengeance against the Height's community. He was not helping Nate the Great resolve his beef with Chaz. Instead, he was using Nathan to score in the gang's battle with the neighborhood. So much for the brotherly love gangs were thought to provide.

"Our crusade to reclaim our homes and heal our hearts has been a huge success, and although we have a long way to go, I know we will be victorious in the end for with God all things are possible!"

With those words the audience erupts in hoots and chaotic clapping. The man at Chastity's side, Father Brinson and the others on stage engulf Chaz in hugs and kisses. Nate wishes he could join them.

"You made it!" yells J-ran over the noise of the vigil vigilantes, startling Nathan.

"What up, Knick Nate?" asks War, sliding on a pair of fingerless gloves.

"You ready to do this, become a real Height's Knight?" adds Raw, punching his open left palm with his clenched right fist.

"Ya'll realize you're talking about stomping a girl, right? Chaz is Chastity . . . a girl," declares Nate, eyebrows raised.

"What is your point?" growls Raw. "We have gangster girls, too. You see her sister Charity was a Knight!"

"Charity was real. We all got a chariot in her honor, to carry her memory," proclaims War, lifting his shirt, exposing his stomach and revealing a tattoo identical to Bryan's.

"Don't tell me you are punking out!" snaps J-ran. "You mean to tell me you are going to let what's under your enemy's clothes keep you from demanding the respect you deserve!"

"This is it," Nathan tells himself, as his heart makes itself at home in the pit of his stomach. *"The bloodshed tonight will be mine because I am not going to let them jump Chaz."*

"Com' on J-ran, forget this butt-face crybaby. Me and War will dance all over cute lil' Chaz. Just say the word!"

Nate charges into Raw full force, his chest bounces hard off the chest of the eldest of the terrible two. War aggressively sandwiches Nathan snuggly against Raw and the twins look to J-ran for instruction.

"Knick Nate, tell me you are not going to let it end like this. Please don't leave me with no other choice but to give the order," insists J-ran, turning up the heat.

"I won't let ya'll jump Chaz. It's not right. She didn't really do anything to me and ya'll have already hurt her enough . . . death is the one thing no one can come back from," Nathan replies, holding his ground.

"What's going on here?" yells Chaz, causing a scene and drawing unwanted attention to the despised Height's Knights. "Get your hands off him! Let him go!" she snaps.

"Make us," barks Raw, backhanding Chaz across her supple dimpled cheek.

Fury illuminates Nathan from the inside out and he tackles Raw to the asphalt and gut punches him relentlessly.

"Oh you have messed up now!" snarls War, diving on top of the brawlers. "Get off my brother, Nate the Snake."

War strikes Nathan with an almost paralyzing kidney shot. But the warrior, the southern chivalry stamped on Nate's soul, would not give in. He sets his mind to defend Chaz and the honor of all of the influential women in his life. Nate battles on.

"What are you looking at?" J-ran roars at Chastity. "Charity was the realest thing that ever came out of your family. You're nothing like your sister!"

"And you're nothing like your brother!" she shouts back at him, caressing her throbbing cheek.

"Chaz! Baby girl, are you straight?" asks Bryan, pushing her to the side and squaring off with J-ran.

"I . . . I . . ." Chastity's words give way to sobbing. Everything she had just campaigned for was unraveling right before her eyes, gang violence. Her father scoops her up and carries her through the crowd, while other vigil attendees pry apart the scrapping boys.

Mr. Isaac focuses all his attention on Bryan and Jyran, who are locked in an intense face-off. "Bryan, son, you are bigger than this. We both know it," he says, voice radiating with wisdom.

"Shut your ol' wrinkled jaw, Pops, before I beat you so bad they have to wire it shut," spits J-ran, without breaking the glare he and B are sharing.

"If you disrespect Mr. Isaac one more time, you are going to get popped in *your* jaw, playground gangster. How you look? Got stupid little boys jumping on a girl! You ain't nothing but a broke down puppet master. Always a follower, hell, you followed me out of the womb. Now you think you are somebody because you lead a group of daycare delinquents!" counters Bryan.

Whoa, hold the phone. Were Nathan's ears deceiving him? Did Bryan just say in no uncertain terms that he and Jyran are brothers, and Jyran was the leader of 'delinquents?' J-ran had told him he usually didn't associate with the younger members of the gang. Dang, the naked truth disclosed.

"Yo B, don't front on me because you weren't man enough to ride it out. You punked out and left the brotherhood to chase after your grooming god and some pipe dream. If you were a real man, Charity would still be alive today."

Jyran has successfully pushed his brother Bryan's button. B draws back with the strength of an ironman to bludgeon his sibling.

However, Mr. Isaac is as swift as he is wise and he catches Bryan's fist just prior to it making contact with bridge of J-ran's nose.

Several more Height's Knights seem to come from nowhere, all of which are underage. Their posture is clear. They are there to back their leader. The crowd of mourners and community supporters show no fear or resistance. They too make it clear where their loyalties lie, with Bryan, Mr. Isaac, Nathan and Chaz.

"B, you know Charity's death was not your fault. You have the scars to prove it. Your brother, God help him, is in need of a serious reality check, the *real* Height's Knights were disassembled by their *real* founder. These phonies should be called *the Lite Mites* because they are out of their league."

"Lite Mites! Lite Mites! Lite Mites!" Nate begins to chant.

"Lite Mites! Lite Mites! Lite Mites! Lite Mites!" The crowd joins in.

With the growing pressure of the crowd, Jryan initiates the retreat of his immature mob.

"Thanks, Mr. Isaac. Sometimes I think the only way my brother is going to have any sense is if I beat some in him. But your wisdom prevailed today. This was a battle not worth fighting," Bryan admits, hugging Mr. Isaac.

"Nathan! You have some explaining to do," demands Nathaniel, shoving his way through the grievous vigil group. "Why did you run off from Sydney like that? And what's this I hear about you hanging around J-ran and his jitterbugs?"

Nate wished his pupils could shoot laser beams so he could pulverize Sydney.

"Don't mug Syd like that. She didn't get you in this mess, you did!" hollers Nathaniel. "Why are you so dirty and why is your lip bleeding?" Finally his father pauses long enough to take in the fullness of his surroundings. Disappointed, he shakes his head in disbelief. "You're back up to your old tricks," he says in a cold calm tone, "You were fighting *once again*, weren't you?"

Tears spill from Nathan's glistening peepers. He gazes at Nathaniel, searching from empathy, but comes up empty handed. Survival in the streets consists of a simple strategy, fight or flight. And since he had already fought, Nate's only option was flight, therefore he bolts.

CHAPTER NINE

Where to, now?

Nathan ran aimlessly until he was overcome with exhaustion. His legs felt like Twizzlers beneath him. He had absolutely no idea where he was. In fact, all he did know was that he couldn't run another step. Leaning against a shop window, he pondered his next move. Rustling sounds from the dark alley a few feet away send Nathan almost sprawling down the subway stairs.

"*No,*"he panics, thinking the shadows in the alley belong to the Height's Knights.

"*Sidekick, I don't ever want you traveling the subway alone,*"his father's words ring out in his ears.

"*You just don't want me, period,*"says Nate to himself, as he pays the attendant. "*You were just waiting for a reason to get rid of me. Now I am no longer your problem, you and stupid snitching Sydney can live happily ever after without me.*"

"Too bad I can't ride the subway all the way back to Georgia, straight to Granny Eva," he says aloud.

Nate wanders the station for a good fifteen minutes, lost in indecision. It reeked of strong urine. "Whoever peed down here needs to drink cranberry juice and more water," he mutters to himself, his stress temporarily giving way to a smile. Nathan had heard Ola Mae say that time and time again about the odor of his own urine.

"Young man, what are you doing?" asks a police officer taking Nate by the arm. "You need to get on about your business. If I didn't know any better, I'd say you're looking for a purse to snatch!"

Nathan gazes up at the officer, but can't get a clear picture of his face for the man's head is illuminated by a bright overhead light.

"I got money!" he declares, snatching his arm away from the police and rummaging through his pocket to retrieve it. "I ain't gotta snatch nobody's purse, thank you very much! I was just waiting on the next train so I can get home to my family. They are waiting on me. It's my birthday and they sent me out to pick up some things so they could set up my *surprise* party," he lies.

"Sorry there, son. I didn't mean to offend you. We've just been having so many muggings by youngsters in this station lately everyone has become a suspect. I'm not going to hold you up any longer. You better get home to your folks. Have a great birthday," replies the cop, a little ashamed for implying Nate was a hoodlum.

"If only you knew," utters Nathan, as he walks towards the platform edge awaiting the next train.

Could Raw and War, J-ran and the rest of the Height's Knight be responsible for the purse snatchings? Sure they could, Nate tells himself. He had listened to numerous 'grab n go' stories from the terrible two.

Rumbling alerted him to the approaching train. Craftily, Nathan steals a peek over his shoulder, pretending he is picking lint off his shirtsleeve. The police officer is still standing there, watching to see him get on the train. With little other choice when the subway car door opens, he steps in. Smugly, he waves at the cop, resisting the urge to gesture good-bye with his middle finger.

Instantly, Nathan affixed on a strange couple. Goth and Punk had collided head on. The guy has a shoulder length ponytail with pink streaks on one side and blue on the other. His female companion was sporting a purple Mohawk. He couldn't even count all the piercings and tattoos he saw between the two. Strange enough, he envied them, twisted as they may appear. At least they had each other, someone who genuinely understood and sympathized with the other's position. Although they may not fit in with what the world calls acceptable, they were accepted by each other.

The weird couple aren't the only people in the car with Nathan. Instead of intruding upon them, he takes a seat near the back. *"One day I'll be accepted... accepted for Nathan... Nathan 'sometimes naughty-sometimes nice' Campbell."* Resting his eyes, Nate reclines and lays his head against the window. *"I'm just going to ride until the subway train runs out of track,"* he thinks.

He heard the adjoining door of the subway car open several times. Hot stale air invited itself inside. He didn't bother opening his peepers to see who accompanied the stifling breeze. Nate figured if it was Nathaniel he would have yoked him from the seat by now, and if it were the Height's Knights he didn't want to see what was coming.

The train made several more stops. From the muffled chatter, it was obvious the subway car had taken on more passengers, but Nathan never observed for himself. There was absolutely no one he wished to see.

"You mind if I cop a squat?" a familiar voice whispers, as a sweet scent acquaints itself with Nate's nose.

"It's a free country," he sighs uninterested and turns his head in the opposite direction of the voice.

"Nathan, don't be like that. Everyone is worried sick about you, searching the streets high and low."

Nate grunts in disbelief.

"I'm serious, Nathan, look at me. There is something I have to say to you. After that, if you want to me go away and forget I ever saw you, I will. I swear on my sister Charity's grave."

Nathan remained unresponsive, having no interest in hearing what Chaz had to say. Deep down, the Nate the Great in him wanted to somehow blame her for his predicament. If she had never moved her backpack his first day of school in the cafeteria, if she would have just spoke to him instead of ignoring him, if only she would have dressed like a girl so he would have known she was a *she* . . .

"Nathan, please," Chastity pleads, moving over to sit next to him. Then she placidly takes his chin in her hand to turn his face towards her own.

The second her sweet smelling flesh touched his, Nathan's body temperature skyrocketed. If there had been a glass thermometer under his tongue, it would have shattered and mercury would have been spewed like hot molten lava. He had never been touched by a girl, at least not on purpose. Chaz was no ordinary girl. She was the prettiest of the pretty. Who would have ever thought she would intentionally touch a tall trouble-making troll like him.

Quaintly, Nate brushes Chaz's hand from his chin, secretly hoping she would instantly reclaim possession of his skin once more. "You have my attention, make it quick. I was resting my eyes," he sighs, trying to be nonchalant.

Nathan was resting his eyes, all right, relaxing in the loveliness before him. Up close, Chaz was even more appealing than Nate had thought humanly possible. Why on earth would someone so beautiful hide it?

"Nathan, I'm sorry. I feel responsible for you getting in trouble. I explained to Mr. Nathaniel how you were trying to protect me. You're *my* hero," Chaz proclaims, placing her soft hand on Nate's knee.

Hero, huh? Nathan liked the sound of that, and for a split second he chose to bask in the thought thereof. Because he knows once he tells Chastity the truth, she was liable to slap his face so hard his head would spin around. In fact, he may be the one in need of rescue or defending.

"Ahem," coughed Nate, clearing his throat and heroic hallucinations. "There's something I need to say to you now. And I want you to promise to hear me out completely before you go off on me."

Puzzled, Chastity takes her hand from Nate's knee and folds her arms across her chest. She was not liking the turn of the tone the conversation. "What do you mean, go off on you?"

"Promise you will hear me out."

Chaz stubbornly nods, accepting the terms of Nathan's confession.

"I am not a hero, especially not *your* hero," he shamefully announces. "I wouldn't have had to defend you if I didn't dislike you?"

Chaz creases her forehead so her eyebrows almost fuse together.

"Just listen, I'm about to explain." Nate pauses to scavenge his mind for the right words. "Where I'm from, I was known as a bully. People never really seemed to like or accept me, so I started giving them a reason not to like me. When I got here, I thought I could start fresh. You were the first person who talked to me here and all you said was, 'I'm Chaz.'

From then on it was like you were ignoring me. Even in shop when Mr. Fields recruited you to teach me the ropes. Remember your one and only rule was, 'look and don't touch.' Don't take this the wrong way but you kids at Hill Street Academy seem like zombie weirdoes. Not talking, walking around like studying robots."

Chastity snickers slightly.

"You're laughing but I'm serious. Anyhow, no one seemed interested in being my friend or interested with the fact that I was alive period. So when I met Raw and War, I jumped at the opportunity to make friends."

Chaz rolls her eyes, *"Raw and War . . . try fake friends!"* she thinks to herself.

"At first I didn't know they were in a gang and, to be real, by the time I found out it didn't matter. They were the only folks in New York besides my dad and the guys at the barbershop who would give me the time of day. J-ran offered me a membership into the Height's knights. I thought it was a good idea. They wanted me in their brotherhood. It felt real good that somebody wanted me, plain old Nate the Great, just as I am.

I considered you a stuck-up, pain-in-my-neck woodworm and I wanted to teach you a lesson. So J-ran suggested I kill two birds with one stone. Stomping you to a pulp after the vigil was going to be my initiation. I would be showing you I demand to be acknowledged and become a full pledge Height's Knight at the same time."

Chastity stared blankly at Nathan. He knew the winds had turned and he was sure she was calling him a few things in her mind, but he'd bet a 'hero' wasn't on the list.

"But at the Wood Wonderland Workshop I realized you were . . . well a girl and there was no way I was beating up a girl."

"You may have tried to but you would have failed!" declares Chaz, unable to hold her peace. "I have a black belt in karate. That's why your fake friends wanted to 'jump' me. They knew they couldn't take me one on one. Speaking of your little buddies, they are locked up waiting to go to boot camp, cause they are forever in trouble."

"I guess you forgot you knew karate when Raw pimp-slapped you?" thinks Nathan to himself.

"Be that as it may, I wasn't raised to hit no girls," he says aloud.

"Sounds like you weren't raised at all," sasses Chaz to herself, still a bit irritated by the notion Nathan had planned to jump on her."

As I listened to you speak at the vigil, I realized how J-ran had tried to play me. Jumping you was not about *my* revenge but *his* against the neighborhood's stand against gangs. He was using me. After the memorial ceremony was over, I told him I wanted no part in the initiation. Raw was willing to step up and carry out the order in my place. But I told him he'd have to go through me to do it. That's when you walked up and, well, you know the rest of the story."

Chaz sits silent for several minutes, just staring at her black Nike tennis shoes. "I guess it's okay, Nathan. In the end, your intentions were good."

Nate exhales sheer relief.

"Just for the record, I think the students at Hill Street Academy are wrapped to tight, too. I've only been going there a year. My mom wanted me out of public school after Charity died. She thought I may seek 'hood life' too if I continued to go to school in the hood. I hate it there, but 'brains over beauty' is my mom's new motto. She's the reason why I dress the way I do and go by Chaz instead of Chastity," Chaz's voice surrenders to sadness.

"My sister . . . my sister, she viewed beauty as a way to rule the world. When the Height's Knights began to break up, she made it her business to become queen of gang mean. Charity wanted to be the one to take the Height's Knights to new heights.

She could have been a real somebody. I mean Charity's pictures—like the one on my shirt—they don't do her justice. My sister's beauty was so rare and raw she could have taken the modeling industry by storm, but she thirsted for power, instant power. Even Bryan fell victim to Charity's beauty. My mom always said Charity wanted to be the first notorious mob mama. You know, female mob boss, and she's probably right. I could see Charity making people kiss her pinky ring or with the nod of her head ordering the murder of someone who had ticked her off."

Chaz pauses, lost in an innocent grin.

"I could go on all day about Charity, but I won't. The point I was trying to make is everyone has a story. And just like a book can't be judged by its cover, neither can I be judged by my clothing. I wasn't ignoring you, I was just telling my story without a word. Sister was beautiful. Sister's beauty led to her thirst for power and control. Sister was killed as a result of her quest to be the queen of gang mean. Mother over-reacted and now surviving child, me, suffers the consequences of mother's paranoia."

"Wow," Nate sighs. "Boy did I read you all wrong. Here I was thinking only people like me had problems and issues."

"Well we beautiful people have problems and issues too," declares Chaz, patting him on the back reassuringly.

"Thanks a lot," Nathan says to himself. *"She just called me ugly on the sly. Seems like her sister Charity wasn't the only one with a beauty ballooned head!"*

"What do you say we get you back home to your father? He is worried out of his mind about you, plus look at it this way, at least your dad encourages you to be you. You don't have to hide beneath your father's fears, like I do my mother's."

"Never thought about it like that, Chaz. Appreciate the insight."

Without uttering another word, Chaz pulled her pink cell phone from her inner jacket pocket and called her father and Nathaniel. She told them she had found Nate safe and sound, and they were on their way to the Heights. And thirty-seven minutes later Nathan was staring his father in the face. Mr. Isaac, Bryan, Sydney and Chaz's parents were all assembled there in the Campbell's small living room.

"Let me speak at you a moment before I head on home," Mr. Isaac tells Nathaniel and the pair disappears into Nathaniel's bedroom.

Chastity's father thanked Nathan for standing up for her and the Davis family journeyed towards their own humble abode. In the meantime, Bryan explained to Nate how he had become so captivated by Chaz's sister Charity's beauty and intrigue that he had remained in the Height's Knights. Although Charity had Jyran a.k.a J-ran wrapped around her little finger, her heart belonged to Bryan.

Charity had always said she needed a man with a spine, with a little buck in him and Jyran, unlike his older brother Bryan, was pure putty in her controlling hands. When the gang began to disperse and Charity made her bid for leader, Bryan battled with leaving the gang. He wanted out of the street life. He had dreams and aspirations that street life could not provide. However, Charity was constantly in his ear reminding him the only way out of a gang was death.

How ironic death was Charity's exit from the Height's Knights. It was apparent to Nate that B was still very unnerved about his girlfriend's death.

"Lil dude, Charity died in my arms." Quiet rapid tears streamed down Bryan's chocolate cheeks. "It was late night, June 27. A day, a night, I'll never forget. Me and Charity met in the park because we thought we would be safe there under the cover of dark. Threats had been made on her life because a rival gang wanted control of the streets, and with the Height's Knights breaking up, they were next in line to run thangs.

Anyway Nate, me and Charity were arguing. She kept asking how it looked for a queen not to have her king reigning right there beside her. And of course I kept pleading with her to leave the Height's Knights, too, so that we could live happily ever after. I'd be her king and she would be my queen and together we would reign on high in our own *legit* kingdom. But Charity wasn't going to budge and I had already begun making efforts to accomplish my dream.

We didn't even hear the car approach. I can't even say that I heard any of the gunshots. I just remember turning, looking over my shoulder long enough to see the flashes of burning gunpowder as countless bullets were fired. It looked almost like fireflies lighting up the night.

I tried to shield Charity with my body. I tackled her to the ground and lay on top of her until the shots stopped. When I rolled off of her I could only hear gurgling. Thick blood was running from the corner of her mouth. I cradled her head and begged her to stay with me. I cried into the night how much I loved her, how much I needed her here with me."

Bryan struggles to control his breathing. Pain had him on the verge of hyperventilating. His nostrils flare like a crazed bull as he fights to inhale through his nose and exhale out his mouth. His voice cracks as he dares to continue.

"She put her blood soaked finger up to my lips to hush my pining." B smiles softly and wipes the fresh tears from his red eyes. "She half whispered, half mouthed, B, tell me I'm beautiful." That's exactly what I did too. And as the life drained from my queen, I felt in my heart that my Charity in her own way had seen the error of her ways, repented for her vanity and only wanted to know that she was still beautiful in spite of her misguided thinking. I still find comfort in thinking about Charity going to Heaven on her very own chariot.

That night with her dried blood still reminding me my girl was gone, I drew the template for this tattoo. By the day of her funeral, many of those who loved Charity were sporting 'Charity's Chariot.' Bryan rolls up his sleeve and lets Nathan get a good look at his tatt in memory of his fallen love.

"I'm sorry for your loss," Nate whispers.

"I'm just happy I was blessed to know her as long as I did. You know, lil man, what's sadder than Charity's death is the fact that word on the street was J-ran was responsible for the shooting. How could you shoot your own brother and the woman you both loved?"

Bryan raises the back of his shirt up above his shoulders to show Nathan the many scars from the shooting.

"Dang, the streets show no love," thinks Nate

Nathaniel and Mr. Isaac finally surface from the back bedroom. Immediately Mr. Isaac takes Nathan in his arms, "I'm proud of you. Today you began to come into your own, your manhood. I know it's overwhelming but remember it's a life-long process. Even a gray-haired old fool like me is still coming to his complete manhood."

"I've been waiting to give you and B a ride home," announces Sydney.

"That Southern charm is another one of your priceless qualities," laughs Mr. Isaac.

"Later, lil dude, later Boss Man," declares Bryan, following Syd and Mr. Isaac to the door.

With everyone gone, the silence was thick, and the words of Mr. Isaac bellow in Nathan's head. *"Real men face the consequences of their actions,"* he thinks to himself.

He takes a deep breath, "Where to, now? . . . Where do we go from here?" Nate asks, ready for the worst.

"I'm going to take you on a journey through your old man's past, so you can make sense of the present and to prep you for your future . . . *our* future."

CHAPTER TEN

Generation of Restoration

Now Nathan was more puzzled than ever. His father's statements were confusing and fascinating all at the same time. However, he did not rush Nathaniel for an explanation. Instead he waited patiently for his dad to explain in his own time.

For quite a few minutes Nathaniel lounges without speaking. He slouches down next to his son and lays his head lazily on the back of the sofa, seemingly resting his eyes. The only indication otherwise is the noticeable motion of Nathaniel's eyeballs rapidly rolling from side to side beneath their lids.

Finally, he speaks void of body movement, "Sidekick, do you remember when I told you I had to grow into my manhood."

Nate remains quiet hanging on his father's every word.

Nathaniel continues, "I told you that you don't go from being a boy to a man overnight and that growing in age does *not* make you a man, right? Remember me saying that?"

"Yes sir," his son replies attentively, clearly recalling the conversation that had taken place between him and his father at the Andrews' residence.

"I also told you back then I wanted everything instantly. I thrived off the thought the world owed me something, something I felt in my heart the only way I was going to get was to take it."

"Um-huh, I remember that too."

Nathaniel straightens his posture, sits upright and peers deep into Nathan's yearning eyes. "Sidekick, I know you have had black history in school and church, right?"

Nate nods yes.

"Then you know being proud and being a black man goes hand in hand, right?"

"I think I understand what you mean."

Nathaniel ponders for a moment for the right words to get his point across to his young son without warping his perception. "Nate, you are a young black man, and I know you have these certain feelings deep inside you, feelings of deep self-respect. You love being black and hate it at the same time sometimes, does that make any sense to you?"

"You mean like, sometimes I love being black because people always say black people run fast and are good athletes but at the same time I hate being black because they think that is all we are good for, kind of like circus freaks. Is that what you mean?"

"Yeah, that is a good example of what I'm talking about. There is no doubt that we come from a dynamic breed. Our ancestors were strong and vigilant, and even though they were slaves, they took great pride in their strength and inner belief in themselves. I believe it was as natural as every breath they took, they *knew* without any doubt whatsoever they would be free and that they would be a great people."

Nathan sat in utter awe of his father's simple yet powerful words. No school or Sunday school teacher had ever broken black history down to him in such a heart wrenching voice. His entire torso is covered with goose pimples.

"Once a black man puts his mind to something, there is absolutely no stopping him. Look at Fredrick Douglas, the Rev. Dr. Martin Luther King Jr., and President, Barack Obama. I'll break it down even further; look at my father, your Grandpa Campbell, one of the first respected black mechanics back home. He wasn't just the black man's mechanic. He was everybody's mechanic. He took pride in the service he provided.

And your Grandpa Jackson, a respected military man who took pride in putting on his uniform and made a permanent mark on the Army. Not by losing his leg in the line of duty, but by the way he carried himself and respected others as he respected himself. Great black men, proud black men . . . men of character and great poise . . . the kind of men that should make all of us proud of the skin we're in.

But sadly enough, some generations seem to lack that character. There are black men who confuse self-respect and pride with arrogance and self-importance. They, just as I did, feel they are owed respect just because their skin is black. But Sidekick, take it from me, respect is earned and not handed out like free samples at a grocery store."

Nathan marveled at how amazing it was that Nathaniel knew exactly how he felt inside. He too had felt he was owed respect, that's why he bullied people. If they weren't going to give him what they owed him, he would take it by force.

"Like I told you, your mother and me, we had big dreams. Your mama just like the great men I spoke about was willing to work and wait for that dream to come to pass. That's the perfect patience of the black woman. They are the ultimate strength of the black man.

Think about how long slavery lasted. Those slaves worked and waited for their dreams of being free to come true. Fredrick Douglas, the freedom fighter, spoke out against slavery and sought an end to the injustice upon black people. Even though his first speech and his second speech seemed to have been in vain, did he quit? No. He continued to work and wait.

Now think about Rev. Dr. Martin Luther King Jr. He dreamed big not only for himself, or black people, for people as a whole. Did he give up after being beaten and mistreated, or after attempts had been made on his life and the lives of those he loved? No, he pressed on, working and waiting for equality, even selflessly giving his life in the end for his dream."

"A dream worth dying for," thinks Nathan to himself. *"I don't know if I want to dream that big."*

"Take President Obama, many black men have dreamt of being president of the United States, he *is* living that dream. And as the first black president, he has earned the respect of many just by going the distance and implementing positive change.

I'm going to get old school on you and even show you the same in your grandfathers. My father, for instance, do you think it was easy for him to get the business of non-blacks?"

Nathan shakes his head no.

"Right you are. There were several years before anyone void of color would even enter my pop's shop without it being a downright emergency. Don't think the blacks were beating down his door either to throw business his way. A lot of them were jealous and said my dad 'thought he was all that.' Yet your Grandpa Campbell worked hard and waited for his business to grow. He didn't demand the respect he felt he deserved as a businessman.

And Willie Jackson, your mother's father, was a diligent soldier. He fought in two wars, received many a medal, but was never promoted in the ranks. He worked and waited, never complaining that he wasn't given the respect he deserved. He wasn't even bitter after he lost his leg and the army discharged him, although honorable, like he was useless to them.

"Now that's something," sighs Nate astonished. "I think I would have been .38 hot if that would have been me."

"Think on this, Nathan, I know you have heard and read about all the things black people, men and women, invented. Yet, if you had not read it or heard about it through black history month, you would have never known such. Those types of things are not broadcast. Do you think those people, our people, are given the respect they have earned as inventors and trendsetters?"

Nate smiles gently as he shakes his head yet again no.

"But yet and still they worked hard waiting for their chance to make the world a better place for everyone, not just blacks."

"We'd be in a mess without some of the things black people invented, like stoplights and air conditioning components. Could you imagine how hot it would be living without air conditioning?" asks Nathan.

"I don't want to think about how hot it would be without it. Boy, am I glad the black person who helped invent the air condition didn't say 'until I get the respect I deserve for my invention, I won't release my work for public use.'"

"Me too!"

"I can go on all day about black people, black men, black pride and black self-respect but I won't. The point I am trying to make is that through perseverance and faith that 'with God all things are possible,' we will eventually get the respect we deserve. Not because we are owed it, but because we earned it by the grace of God. When things are of God, Sidekick, folks have no other choice but to acknowledge such.

Back in the day, after you were born I didn't acknowledge that. When your mother died, I was lost and the thought that the world owed me respect grew like a brushfire within me. I was determined to take what I was owed. I wandered as far away from the South as my few saved bucks would take me, and I ended up here in New York. The ignorance in me thought a black man would never get the respect owed him living in the South.

How stupid of me, when my own father's business had proven otherwise. Anyhow, I set out on a ruthless quest motivated by what I thought was pride but in hindsight I see was arrogance. It's a thin line between pride and arrogance, son, so you have to very careful in your thinking."

Tears weld up in Nathaniel's eyes as he reveals the reason for his absence in Nate's life. "Nathan, *I* founded the *original* Height's Knights. It was the fruit of my arrogance. I even handpicked Bryan to be my number one wingman. The power of leading a gang fueled my pursuit of 'taken respect.' People didn't have to like me, but I'd be damned if they weren't going to respect me. I ruled with an iron fist and took everything I thought should have been mine.

I lived in a high-rise loft and drove fancy imported cars. I wore the best clothes, shoes and jewelry that stolen money could buy. However, no matter how many people feared me, I never felt it was enough. You know why, son?"

Nate murmurs the word no, still dumbfounded that his father, his hero, was the founder of a gang. The same gang he almost joined.

"Just like folks can easily confuse pride and arrogance, I confused fear for respect. The two couldn't be more different. Anyhow, son, one afternoon, my crew and I were barbequing in the courtyard at the Height's apartments. Even though none of us lived there anymore, we still hung out there. Most of the tenants were too afraid to say anything to us so we pretty much had run of the place.

That particular day I got into it with an older man. Me and this cat had had run-ins before because for whatever reason he was not scared of me or the gang power I possessed. So we had words or whatever and the old man got the best of me in front of my boys. He made me look bad and I couldn't have that. I couldn't have my street credibility challenged by some old crow. That would be like throwing my respect, the respect I had *taken*, right out the window.

So as that old man walked off, heading towards a concrete

picnic table where he and several other snow capped brothers played chess daily, I pulled out my gun."

Nathaniel stares with empty eyes at the arm of the sofa. Nate swallows hard, tingling inside out of anticipation.

In a mellow but hypnotic tone, Nathaniel finds the courage to continue. "I called the old cat's name, there's no honor in shooting a man in the back. Truth be told, son, there is no honor in shooting a man period, even in cases of self-defense. As I'm sure you heard your Me'ma say a million or so times, death is the only thing you can't come back from. Anyhow, as he turned around I raised the weapon. The old man looked me dead in the eye and never flinched.

There was no fear to be found in his gaze. In my heart I know if he had shown a mere hint of fear I would have never pulled the trigger but he didn't. He was fearless and denied my arrogance its respect. Therefore, I emptied the clip in my gun. Only two rounds hit the old man though. Your dad was a bad shot."

Nathaniel pauses just long enough to redirect his gaze from the sofa's arm to his son's eyes. He knows the question on the tip of Nathan's tongue is whether or not the old man lived or died.

"Sidekick, in slow motion I watched that old man fall to the ground and all my homies scatter in the wind like autumn leaves. But I couldn't flee, no matter how hard B tugged at my arm I refused to run. In fact I ordered him to go on without me. I had to look into that old man's face one last time.

As I towered over him I couldn't believe my eyes. I had to get down on my knees beside him because I just knew my pupils were lying to me. Kneeling there beside the man I had just shot, a man I had just put two bullets in for no legitimate reason, I was disappointed and bewildered all at the same time. He didn't plead for his life nor whimper in pain. Instead he glared at me in defiance. There was still no fear or respect for my callousness in his eyes.

That day, that moment I had been defeated and not because I was arrested, but because I had been denied what I thought was mine; denied even though I had tried to take it at gunpoint, respect. I felt less than a man and ashamed. That night as I lay on a metal mattress-less bunk bed, I cried. I cried tears of anger and self-hatred. I cried tears of regret and hopelessness. I cried tears of loneliness. You see, even though, I was constantly surrounded by people,—my crew mainly—I was empty inside.

Take it from me, Sidekick, true pride and self-respect doesn't leave you feeling empty. It fills you up with encouragement and diligence. It makes you keep on keeping on even when it seems there is no point in doing so. It honors your heart and blesses your dreams. It doesn't devalue others or make you feel worthless. It is the adrenaline that made the proud black men before us stand tall and continue to work towards there dreams and aspirations, *patiently awaiting* the respect they *earned.*"

"*Wow, that's deep,*" Nate cooed subconsciously.

"I toiled all night long, wrestling with the demon within me, my arrogance. Your Me'ma used to say all the time it's darkest just before dawn and that night her words became clear. I had to reach the lowest part of my life, the darkest hour in my life before dawn could breakthrough. I had lost my wife, left my son and mother, moved hundreds of miles away from the only home I had ever known. I had just shot someone. I was locked up. I had finally admitted to myself that I was lonely and empty . . . it couldn't get any darker than that.

I called out to God to restore me, restore my generation and remove the shame I had brought to the Campbell name. I pined for Him to fix me and right my wrongs. I asked Him over and over again why had He forsaken me and left me alone in this world without Abigail, my angel on earth. Do you know what God showed me, as if it were a picture show?" Nathaniel asks his son, wondering if maybe he too had encountered a vision from the Lord.

"No sir, what did God show you?" inquires Nate, his ears perked up like a hyper puppy.

"God showed me that He had not left me but I had left from him. Taking respect had replaced Him in my life. I had become so wrapped up in demanding the fast respect I thought I was owed, I no longer honored the Almighty, nor did I trust Him to bring my dreams to pass. I was going to do it myself and in record time.

Just like a lot of young boys today, I thought the more money, expensive clothes, bling-bling jewelry, tricked out cars and homes I had, the more respect I would get. But the more worldly idols I acquired, the less room there was for God in my life. And I call all that stuff idols because I had come to worship them and the power, the false sense of *respect* they brought me."

Looking around their humbly furnished and decorated apartment, Nathan struggles to imagine his father ever living the life of luxury.

"Don't get what I'm saying twisted. There is nothing wrong with having nice things but they should never replace God. The bible says 'seek ye first the kingdom of Heaven and the desires of your heart shall be given unto you.' I went about my quest for respect the wrong way. I tried to exalt myself before it was my time, and trust me, son, I learned the hard way, from God comes promotion and in His timing will all things come to pass. That night I gave my life to Jesus and begged him to help me right my wrong, no matter how long it took."

"So you didn't go to prison for shooting that man?"

"Oh yes, Sidekick, I went to prison. Just because I gave my life to Christ didn't mean I didn't have to pay for my crime. I did eight and a half years in prison, including eighteen months in County lockup. However, I am not bitter, even though it is sad to say had I not shot that old man I would have never began to come into my manhood nor would I have ordered the dispersing of the Height's Knights."

"Did the old man die?" asks Nathan, not really sure he wants to know the answer to his question.

It was hard enough to think of his father as a gang founder. Therefore, Nate knows it would undoubtedly be an even tougher pill to swallow if his father was a murderer as well.

"No the man didn't die. In fact, he tried for many years to visit me in prison, but shame wouldn't let me face him. He even had Bryan trying to talk me into seeing him. Bryan visited me religiously, keeping me informed about how the gang had taken on new life under different leadership, and he always made mention of the old cat I shot. However, he never pressured me, out of admiration.

One visitation day as I walked into the visiting room there was my boy B, but he was not alone. The old man was planted right beside him. I wanted to turn around and haul butt back to my prison dormitory but something funny happened. I realized I had mad respect for the old man whose life I'd tried to take.

It takes a strong man, a principled man, a God fearing man to forgive someone who wounded you, especially physically. Yet here was this man of great character reaching out to the very hoodlum who had permanently scarred him. He embraced me with the strength of our ancestors. He counseled me with the wisdom of our forefathers. He forgave me with the mercifulness of Jesus and he loved me with the heart of God. He became my breathing model of a proud, self-respecting black man.

He kept visiting me from that day forward. He took me under his wing and nurtured my growth as I came into my *true* manhood. He taught me by example. He gave me the courage when I got out of prison to straighten my life up and relentlessly fight the monster I had created, the Height's Knights. He helped me start my business. He became my mentor. Nathan, *he* . . . is Mr. Isaac."

"Whoa, my dad shot Mr. Isaac," Nate says to himself, trying to wrap his mind around such a thought. *"Dad's life story could be a B.E.T movie of the week."*

"Now, Sidekick, I don't even think about respect, yet I know each day that I am earning it. I'd be lying through my teeth if I said the people around here welcomed me back in the community with open arms. They would have been fools to. But once they saw that my victim had given me a second chance, plus the fact that I was fearless in my crusade to right my wrong, and take down not only the gang I had founded, but any other gang within our ten-twenty mile radius, they began to warm up to me.

I've dedicated my life to giving back. I took Bryan under my wing like Mr. Isaac did me. I mentor and counsel any child willing to receive me and the help I offer. I work hard and wait patiently and expectantly for my efforts to make a positive difference in this community. I realize, Sidekick, that the *active* contents of a man beat the heck out of his potential. All along I contained the characteristics of a respectable man."

Overwhelmed with understanding for his father's absence, engulfed by justified respect for his dad and the many steadfast, strong, respectable black men before him, and re-assured with hope for his own future because of Nathaniel's uncut confession, Nate not only embraces his dad but embraces the present. Whereas words had abandoned him, Nathan was not at a loss for tears. The tears of a young black man finding his own true pride and self respect, a young black man maturing not only physically but in his thinking as well.

"I'm proud of you dad and instead of being the worm that spoiled the big apple, I want to be the apple of your eye."

"Mission accomplished. You've been the apple of my eye since the very day you were born," wept Nathaniel sincerely. "All I ask is that you be the best *you*, you can be."

The pair hug with great emotion and when they break the bond that binds them, all is well.

"Superhero?"

"Yes trusty, Sidekick?"

"You were restored right?"

"By the grace and mercy of God, yes son, I claim restoration."

"And you are doing everything in your power to restore the community you damaged, right?"

"Correct."

"I want to restore a wrong I caused too," professes Nate.

"And what wrong would that be?" asks Nathaniel, thinking his son's request probably involves Chaz or school.

"Promise you'll hear me out before you decide," declares Nathan, condemning his father to silence.

"I promise," Nathaniel replies a bit reluctantly.

Nate inhales deeply. "I know you have said time and time again that I did not kill my mama. She had a weak heart that nobody including her knew about."

Nathaniel nods in agreement but honors his promise by not speaking a word.

"Anyhow, dad, a small part of me still feels guilty. I kinda feel like if it wasn't for me the thread that held you and Grandpa Jackson together would still exist and there would be hope for you and him to like each other."

Nathaniel can only raise his eyebrows at that notion.

"So since I accidentally caused a bigger rift between you two, I think it's my responsibility to restore the generation gap. I want to kinda be a blood bridge between two strong, respectable black men. What do you think?"

Nathaniel leans forward, fully alert, and clasps his hands together, "What did you have in mind, Sidekick?"

One statement at a time, Nathan reveals his plan for restoration, and over the next month or so he and his father put the plan in motion. Late one evening, Nate receives a phone call from his Grandpa Jackson. They talk for hours rambling on and on as if they had been acquainted forever. Both Nathan and his dad are surprised when Willie Jackson ends the call by asking to speak to Nathaniel.

"Hello," says Nathaniel, his voice burly and unyielding.

Nathan's heart races as he tries to imagine what his grandfather is saying on the other end.

"Yes sir . . . yes sir . . . yes sir," was all Nathaniel says before placing the phone on the charger.

"Dad, don't leave me in suspense. What did he say?" implores Nate in anticipation.

"He said he looks forward to meeting you in two weeks!"

Nathan jumps up and down ecstatic. "Are you serious?"

"I would never joke about something like that."

Needless to say, Nathan floated on pure unbridled eagerness for the next thirteen days. On that fourteenth day, the day of truth, standing in his grandfather's front yard he asked Nathaniel to pinch him, for he had to be dreaming. A baldheaded brown skinned man hobbles from inside the house onto the front porch with the help of a metal walker.

Porches were one of the Southern delicacies Nathan had come to miss while living in the city. They were as country as hand-churned ice cream, and as comforting as a seemingly ten pound hand-stitched quilt on a cold winter's night.

Nate's nerves began to breakdance as he sized up his Grandpa Jackson. Willie Jackson's beard was precisely trimmed and white gray. His head was smoothly shaven with absolutely no hint of stubble. If he had to guess, Nate would say his grandfather shaved his head with a straight razor. The old man's stature was not handicapped by his missing extremity. He still soared, upright and unmovable. And his clothes were pressed stiffer than any drycleaner could even fathom. Before Nathan and Nathaniel stood a *real* soldier.

"Don't just stand there," he chuckles, his voice deep as a cobblestone well.

Nathan grabs his father's hand and jerks him towards the ramp that intersected the porch.

"You are one find looking young man, Nathan," declares Willie Jackson, peering at his grandson through glazed eyes. "I can see my Abigail in you."

To possess some likeness of his mother made Nate feel closer to her memory. Willie Jackson cuddles his grandson, the only living proof outside of himself that his beloved Abigail had ever existed. As Nate indulged in his grandfather's arms and the smell of Old Spice, he couldn't help but wonder how many times had his mother been cradled in those very same limbs.

"Nathaniel, I was sorry to hear about Ola Mae's passing. You and she have raised one fine boy. Abby would be proud," proclaims Mr. Jackson, for the very first time honored to have him as a son-in-law.

"Thank you, Mr. Jackson. That means so much coming from you," Nathaniel replies, firmly shaking his father-in-law's aged hand.

"Ain't no point in standing round here all afternoon. Let's go on 'round back so I can show ya'll where my Abby is buried." Willie Jackson aligns his walker with the porch wall and takes hold of Nathan and Nathaniel for support as he walks.

In the backyard under a large oak tree with a tire swing was Abigail Jackson-Campbell's grave.

"I see you made good use of the present we sent you," laughs Nate, truly and without bias admiring Chaz's wood workmanship.

Nathaniel had gifted Mr. Jackson the bench swing he had won at the Wood Wonderland Workshop, kind of as a peace offering.

"It sits real good," he announces, smiling to reveal his profound crow's feet.

Just inches from the slab covering his mother's grave, Nathan takes the space between his father and grandfather, the blood bridge of restoration firmly implanted. Tightly holding the hand of each, he reads his mama's headstone, "Here lies Abigail Jackson-Campbell, an angel long before she ascended into heaven. Your light shone on earth only for a season . . . but your memory lives on forever in our hearts. Precious daughter, devoted wife, and blessed mother rest in peace."